I0638214

THE
BOLIVIAN
SAILOR

DONALD DEWEY

MILFORD
HOUSE

an imprint of Sunbury Press, Inc.
Mechanicsburg, PA USA

MILFORD HOUSE

an imprint of Sunbury Press, Inc.
Mechanicsburg, PA USA

NOTE: This is a work of fiction. Names, characters, places and incidents are the product of the author's imagination or are used fictitiously, and any resemblance to actual persons, living or dead, business establishments, events or locales is entirely coincidental.

Copyright © 2018 by Donald Dewey
Cover Copyright © 2018 by Sunbury Press, Inc.

Sunbury Press supports copyright. Copyright fuels creativity, encourages diverse voices, promotes free speech, and creates a vibrant culture. Thank you for buying an authorized edition of this book and for complying with copyright laws by not reproducing, scanning, or distributing any part of it in any form without permission. You are supporting writers and allowing Sunbury Press to continue to publish books for every reader. For information contact Sunbury Press, Inc., Subsidiary Rights Dept., PO Box 548, Boiling Springs, PA 17007 USA or legal@sunburypress.com.

For information about special discounts for bulk purchases, please contact Sunbury Press Orders Dept. at (855) 338-8359 or orders@sunburypress.com.

To request one of our authors for speaking engagements or book signings, please contact Sunbury Press Publicity Dept. at publicity@sunburypress.com.

ISBN: 978-1-62006-209-8 (Trade paperback)

Library of Congress Control Number: 2018937203

FIRST MILFRED HOUSE PRESS EDITION: March 2018

Product of the United States of America
0 1 1 2 3 5 8 13 21 34 55

Set in Bookman Old Style
Designed by Crystal Devine
Cover by Lawrence Knorr
Edited by Lawrence Knorr

Continue the Enlightenment!

For Bryan and Ibelice

CURRICULUM VITAE

Not everybody is cut out to be a teacher. I learned this the hard way.

One night at my father-in-law's house, somebody said something over the veal cutlet, somebody else answered, and I thought they both had a point. A couple of months later, I was standing in a Long Island classroom trying to get my mouth around my name for 33 college juniors. I managed my name, even wrote it on the blackboard without making a mistake, then turned back into my first titter. As the wiseguy sitting in the last row said for everybody: "Is there another way to spell Paul Finley?"

That got a few louder laughs, and I clung to them: Once the laughter stopped, I was going to have to say something coherent about the jiffy course entitled Practical Problems of Law Enforcement. Then and there I would have preferred going up against a shooter in an alley.

Before my teaching debut, I hadn't been in a school building since graduating from Adelphi University. After graduation, I'd drifted through a series of jobs that put a minimal value on thinking. Sometimes I think it was only to show I could still tell the difference between a rectangle and triangle that I took the exam for the Nassau County police force. Eventually, I reached first-grade detective. For almost 12 years I was the one you saw on the news walking across parking lots with prisoners, coming out of courtrooms with prisoners, and, every once in a while, trying to fudge why I didn't have any prisoners. Overall, I did a pretty good job and didn't need a few citations and plaques to think so.

I might not have been Hall of Fame material, but I was a pretty regular all-star.

All of that went down the tubes five Christmases ago when my wife Jennifer and six-year-old daughter Susan were killed in a car crash. For a long time, I blamed myself for their deaths because they were killed going home from my father-in-law's after an end-less Christmas dinner during which I had drunk myself into the guest bed. My father-in-law Joe Carroll matched his guilt to mine for not having insisted I get up and drive my family home and for having gotten into an argument with Jennifer that had sealed her decision to brave icy roads instead of staying the night with me.

The accident made me no good for a lot of things, includ-ing the Major Cases division in Mineola. When a police shrink recommended I take a leave of absence, I first thought she was overreacting; two weeks away from the job, I decided she had un-der-reacted. I just didn't want to go back. I didn't give two cents if every homeowner in Nassau got murdered, robbed, or torched out of hearth and garage. I had lost mine, so why couldn't other people lose theirs, too?

It was in this same why-not spirit that I found myself in a saloon one night accepting a job as an investigator for Gramercy Insurance. Most of the work was interviewing incompetent or mercenary doctors, comparing their evasiveness to the accusa-tions of aggrieved patients, and standing back while Gramercy used my reports for determining if a settlement was in order. From there it was a short step to the other standbys of a private investigator—the other woman, the other man, the father who had skipped town with child support payments, the wife who had disappeared instead of delivering the kids to dad for the weekend. It was pretty banal stuff and appealed to me precisely because it was. When I needed help on a hard trace, I only had to drop in on my former colleagues in Mineola, put up with 10 minutes of cracks about professional freeloaders, and look like I enjoyed them before walking out with my information. Since I had moved into my father-in-law's house in Garden City to bind our misery as a 24-hour-a-day commitment, my expenses were minimal. I converted his basement into the international headquarters for

Finley Investigations, seldom had reason to lay big bills on a restaurant table, and couldn't find the energy to travel much further than to Mets games. As for women, they were doctors, dentists, clients, litigants, cops, receptionists, secretaries, storekeepers, actresses at the Multiplex, and anchors on the 11:00 news; none of them applied for the position of Paul Finley's lover.

You get the picture: It was the Self-Pity Years. But all good things come to an end. My Waterloo was a murder case that ricocheted off every third mover and shaker in Nassau and Suffolk counties. Although there was some debate over who had been responsible for what, and what any of it had to do with the price of instant coffee, there seemed to a consensus that the stickier metaphysical questions might have been avoided altogether if Paul Finley hadn't kept stumbling around and making too much noise for the federal prosecutor to ignore. In short order, I lost my rabbi at Gramercy Insurance, then Gramercy Insurance itself. Because I had shown distrust of the county prosecutor's office and gone to the feds, I became *persona non grata* at key record offices. My ex-colleagues at Major Cases, some of whom had been tainted by the murder case, made it clear I would be welcome again in their offices only when I came by to be booked. It was only because *Newsday* made a third-page stink on a slow news day that threats to lift my license went no further than that.

I don't lay all this out as a gripe. Some people might even see my brush with Authority as a life-affirming experience. It certainly yanked me out of my humdrum ways with Gramercy and ended lingering illusions about my old job in Mineola (if I didn't want to be a cop, I shouldn't have counted on being an ex-cop, either). There was also the small matter of rediscovering a small artery or two in my body once I had told some of Nassau's Worthiest to go to hell. I hadn't quite died that night with Jennifer and Susan, after all. I could still get some blood to my heart.

And let's not stop at the moral, psychological, and physiological considerations. Under the fallout from the *persona non grata* Finley I found the courage to sit down with my father-in-law one evening and ask for a $5000 loan. I needed the money to get an apartment of my own and end the misery-loves-company arrangement we had tolerated far too long. The Professor (the nickname Joe Carroll had picked up for his pontificating about history on and off the campus) reacted as though I wanted to give him the $5000. If I'd waited any longer, he told me, he would have changed the locks on the door and left the money with my clothes on the front stoop; he too had grown weary of wallowing in the past. Three weeks later, he bought a smaller house only a couple of blocks away from his old campus and I rented an apartment in the Bay Ridge section of Brooklyn. It took him two months to close on the place he had been living in for 30 years and another month after that for me to agree to be the trustee for the sale money. "If you don't go along," he threatened me at one point, "I'm going to leave it all to the Scientologists. You choose."

Another consequence of my involvement in the Long Island murder case was a second adolescent rush of hormones: I was finally able to stop seeing every woman through the memory and excuse of my 12 years with Jennifer. First, there was a magazine editor I met in front of my new Brooklyn building, then the owner of a saloon on the corner of my block. Neither of them believed in me as a long-term investment, I was relieved to have regained the status of even a short-term investment, and there was more melancholy than grief when we started finding reasons for not seeing each other. Would I ever be capable of more? I didn't know, but I had hopes every so often that my acne would clear up eventually.

As for Finley Investigations, it boomed with the move from Garden City to Brooklyn. Instead of no cases a month, I came up with two-and-a-half within two months. The first one was a four-day surveillance of a Park Place bodega in Prospect Heights; my job was to alert a block association when a slumlord showed up to harass the intimidated old woman who ran the store. The second assignment was a telephone call or two to check out the bonafides of a superintendent who might or might not have invented his garbage-collecting credentials to qualify for an apartment house job on Fort Hamilton Parkway. The half was a cop's wife, a friend of my magazine editor friend, who wanted me as a veteran of the ambiance to name all the places where her husband might be making it with his new woman partner. The slumlord never showed up, the super had lied, and I gave the cop's wife an insider's list that started with a motel and ended with the other woman's apartment. My clients were beside themselves in gratitude for my industry, and I piled up almost $450.

It wasn't much, and it wasn't a living, either.

That was why I listened that evening at the Professor's supper table when two of his academic protégés went on about how Adelphi's political science department was looking for somebody to deliver lectures twice a week to undergraduates on the Practical Problems of Law Enforcement. The idea was that tomorrow's lawmakers should be exposed for at least two hours a week to something besides thirteenth-century theories on government. I needed all of half a second to remember that Nassau County had thousands of cops, ex-cops, and bank guards who could have done the job, to realize why I had been invited to the dinner, and to smirk that all those cops, ex-cops, and bank guards didn't have an in with the university like the Professor.

My contact at the political science faculty was Phil Ortega, a second-generation Colombian, an expert on Latin American affairs, and (from what I was told) the man in America most eager to meet me. A few days after the Professor's dinner I drove back out to Garden City for what I had supposed was going to be a job interview. What it turned out to be was Ortega getting me to tell war stories over watery coffee in the university cafeteria. My only flub in more than an hour was to ask if he had any guidelines in mind for the course; he looked dismayed that I hadn't realized my street stories were the course and that merely showing up to meet him had gotten me the job.

Now granted 99.9 percent of the people in my position would have recognized a gift horse for what it was and driven back home warming up their Favorite Busts. But in case you haven't guessed by now, I've never been especially good at recognizing gift horses. For one thing, after I'd finished feeling grateful to the Professor and his friends for jumping me to the head of the line, I was still just holding a contract paying me a miserable $2100 for 28 hours of blather spread out over four months. That might have been more than was to be made keeping an eye on Park Place bodegas, but not so much more that I could start planning a vacation to Tahiti. Then there was the other problem—the Finley Problem.

I didn't care what Ortega had figured. I had no intention of strolling into a classroom, bullshitting for an hour, then just strolling out again. If they wanted a course on the practical problems of law enforcement, that was what they were going to get. So, I went to work. By the time I walked into that classroom the first time, I was as ready to talk about the conflicting jurisdictions of the FBI, the state police, and the park rangers in Montana as I was about Finley's Greatest Cases. I was also ready to admit that the Professor, Ortega, and their circle had pooled all their wiles to produce the most impractical person in the Greater Metropolitan Area for their course on the practical problems of law enforcement.

Needless to say, I wouldn't be recounting any of this unless it had a relatively happy ending. Once over the class's mock appreciation of my ability to spell my name, I made the consoling discovery that the 20-year-old juniors sitting in front of me were really just warm, sympathetic pricks who expected me to provide value for their tuition money. I decided I could live with that condition, and launched my new career by telling them that retail outlets were just bluffing with signs claiming they reserved the right to inspect packages. That got the attention of their shoplifting neurons, and I went on from there to all the non-existent laws that were being enforced by people who had come across them in their private penal codes. By the third or fourth session, we had established what the Professor called a *modus vivendi* and what I called earning my $2100.

That was the good news. The better news, at least until the Bolivian sailor came along, was that my avocation enlarged my social circle beyond Cynthia and the skels who hung out at her corner bar. It didn't take the Professor long to exploit his renewed proximity to the campus by emitting a patriarchal glow for evening get-togethers with former teaching disciples, their wives or husbands, and the odd graduate student. After so many years of hibernating in the old house with the TV set and our guilts about Jennifer and Susan, it was dismaying to finish up one of my night classes and go over to the Joe Carroll Salon. At 75, the Professor was back in academic business with a vengeance, getting run-downs on this one and that one, then explaining to his informants why this one and that one had always been assholes—and he had the parallels from the War of the Roses and Desert Storm to show how. It was a change, I can now admit, I resented at first. Had it been *me* who had been such a wet blanket on his spirits? Or, vice versa, what about his daughter and grandchild—had they suddenly become less important to him than the latest gossip from the quadrangle?

Right: I had obviously moved a few more demons of my own than I'd realized to Brooklyn. I got over my resentment.

Nobody was more of a regular at the Professor's gatherings than Phil Ortega. Alone or with his glum-faced wife Barbara, Ortega was a fixture on the old man's living room rug, disputing Carroll's exaggerations with a weight that seemed totally out of proportion to the occasion. As I found out pretty quickly, the Colombian was as close to an international VIP academic as Adelphi had. When he wasn't administering the political science faculty and conducting special postgraduate seminars, he was attending world conferences, writing Op-ed pieces for the *Times*, and serving as a consultant for companies with holdings in Chile and Venezuela. I can say it now because I thought it then: There was something that just didn't fit about Ortega sitting on the Professor's floor and debating the old man about the hypocrisies of capitalist democracies.

Of course, even back then I had my theories. My favorite idea was me—that the ivory tower intellectual couldn't get enough of my war stories. Given Ortega's standing, I was also sure he knew more about my earlier troubles with the Nassau County heavy-weights than he had let on. That proved to be the case. One night, after he had sipped more wine than usual, he told me he'd heard "a lot of people hate your guts." But just as I was wondering if that was a prelude to announcing he had lost interest in the practical problems of law enforcement, he gave me a salmon-mouthed smile and said he'd found a hole in his budget for extending my tenure for another semester for an additional couple of hundred dollars.

When in doubt, let bafflement reign. Before long the Professor and I were guests at the Ortega place in Sea Cliff for a four-hour dinner, Phil was calling me on weekends to clarify some point about police procedures that seemed to apply to an article he was writing about the constabulary in Caracas, and I was a logical fourth for evenings when a cousin of Barbara's or colleague of Ortega's showed up in New York for a few days. It might have been all apples and oranges, but I saw no reason not to focus on the fruit salad instead of on its individual ingredients. When the Ortegas took a working vacation in Colombia over the Christmas holidays, they even offered me the use of their place. I had no reason for chilling my bones in Sea Cliff instead of banging on the radiator in Bay Ridge, but I appreciated the offer. I even wished I could feel as much of a friend toward them as they had decided to feel toward me.

Then the Bolivian sailor came along, and I had to forget about the Ortegas to concentrate on some truly practical problems of law enforcement.

ONE

The Bolivian sailor walked into my life in the form of a Manhattan detective named Masterson. I was on my living room couch one night going over case files when Masterson rang my bell. In the time it took me to close the door behind him and work into my loafers, I had two candidates from my files as a half-story about to be closed at my expense. Killed, arrested, or fled the country, they had escaped my expense account.

Naturally, I was wrong.

"Mr. Finley, are you familiar with a Victor Paz?"

The name sounded familiar—but only until I thought of the capital of Bolivia. "I don't think so," I said, cutting off thoughts of old Hollywood character actors. "Who is he?"

Masterson put my question aside for a survey of the living room. What he saw was A&S Traditional—furniture fit for an aunt and uncle who sometimes put their feet up. "The card in the bell downstairs says Finley Investigations. That your business, Mr. Finley?"

"Right. Is there some reason I should know this Paz?"

"He seemed to know you."

The *seemed* was meant to impress, and it did. "I take it he's not with us anymore?"

Masterson smiled tolerantly. Despite a thick mustache and enormous green marbles for eyes, there was something fundamentally blank about his face, as though its individual features had been afterthoughts. "Ever with the Department, Mr. Finley?"

"Nassau. Major Cases."

He nodded like somebody who liked his cops on Long Island only when they commuted from there to the job in the city. "Well, I'm going to have to ask you to drive into Manhattan with me. We have an ID problem, and looks like only you can help us with it."

"Right now?"

"It'd be a help."

"But I don't know the guy!"

"Maybe it's someone you know by some other name. Happens all the time, even out on the Island, right?"

I knew I was looking at the border of Masterson's tact, but I didn't relish a useless trip from Bay Ridge to Manhattan at nine o'clock, either. "Maybe if you'd describe this Paz, I could save us a false alarm."

"Got me," he said, redoing the top button of his overcoat. "I never saw him. Just going after the groceries, you understand?"

I had been a cop, so I was supposed to understand the lingo. And shut up and go for a useless ride.

* * *

Masterson said little on the drive into Manhattan. When he did open his mouth, it was to gripe about other drivers or the city's failure to build another dozen bridges between Brooklyn and Manhattan. If nothing else, he convinced me I *was* only groceries for him, that as soon as he dropped me off at the morgue, he was going to go on to bigger things than Paul Finley and Victor Paz. And sure enough, as soon as we pulled up in front of a blue brick building on First Avenue and 31st Street, he was down to jabbing a thumb at the entrance. "Go in and ask for Sergeant McGill. They'll take care of you from there."

I got out of the car to be taken care of, and to curse my tactical error in not driving myself in after him. The wild goose chase would have been bad enough on its own, but then there was going to be the endless trip back home on the **R** train. As I pushed through the glass doors of the Bellevue annex and went over to the receptionist, I couldn't even think of anything pertinent about the experience for my next Adelphi class.

Sergeant McGill was waiting in a plastic chair behind the reception desk. She was a stubby, thirty-something blonde in black corduroys and a green bomber jacket. Her tight smile said she was willing to be friendly, but her clinical stare said she wasn't used to drawing boilerplate duties. I had seen her look on Ellen Miles, my partner in Major Cases in Mineola: DON'T TREAD ON ME. In Mineola, I had made the mistake of treading; I didn't intend repeating my mistake.

By the time we had taken the elevator downstairs and entered the viewing room, McGill had gotten everything out of me Masterson might have gotten if he had been interested enough to ask. No, I didn't know any Victor Paz. No, I hadn't forgotten a Victor Paz from my days as a cop or private investigator on the Island, from my Bay Ridge cases, or even from my evening classes or Cynthia's saloon. No, I didn't have any Latin friends who might have been a common denominator.

"That's weird," she decided, as the morgue attendant walked toward us. "So how would your name come up?"

"I have a better question. How *did* it come up?"

She didn't look like she was going to enlighten me on that point anyway, but the attendant's wave for us to follow him saved her breath. We trooped down a silent corridor that might have been lighted by the same people responsible for the House of the Night Creatures at the Bronx Zoo. I almost walked up McGill's calves when she stopped abruptly before a curtained window. She was obviously acquainted with the place, and I would have been happy to leave it at that. But some familiar hives tickled at my elbows, too, as we waited for the attendant to go in a door and make a formal presentation. "Something wrong?" she asked.

Several answers occurred to me, including my annoyance that she hadn't acted convinced about a single thing I'd told her and that the last bodies I'd identified had been Jennifer's and Susan's. I settled for shaking my head and trying to look more scientific about what I was going to see.

The attendant parted the window curtain to his holding room. There were six or seven bodies under sheets on gurneys spread around the chamber. He hesitated a second to get a nod from

McGill before he raised the sheet from the corpse closest to the window. I knew the hesitation had been for McGill to be ready to study my face at seeing the body.

Victor Paz had been in his late 20s or early 30s. He had a razor chin and a pudgy nose in a moon face and had let his black hair grow down over the tops of his ears. The rise of his feet under the sheet said he had been no more than 5'7" on the thin side. With his hands covered I couldn't begin to guess at what he had done for a living. A small light went off in the back of my head: I was disappointed I *hadn't* known him.

"Never saw him before."

The trouble with anticipating what you're going to say is you don't sound persuasive even to yourself. I'd been sure I'd never known a Victor Paz and had already heard myself saying as much, but all McGill heard was the rehearsal. "Maybe you should look again."

"Sergeant, I can stand here all night and I still won't know him. What happened to him?"

Naughty questions again, but this time she decided to move on to a bigger test for me. "He was shot twice in the back," she said evenly. "Looks like a silencer. So, a professional job."

I nodded because I didn't have anything better to do. The attendant on the other side of the window was still waiting for me to change my story. "Okay, so now it's a murdered Victor Paz I never heard of."

McGill tried not to show she was a bad sport. She nodded something like thanks to the attendant, then started back out toward the bleary lighting of the elevator well. "You can understand the dilemma we have," she said, none of Masterson's *Mr. Finley* even implied in her chilly tone. "The least we can do is account for the bodies."

"That's a joke, right?"

"If you don't mind, I'd like you to talk to my boss for a minute. He was hoping you could help us out."

"I still might if I knew how my name came up."

"Mr. Paz had a telephone address book," she sighed, pressing for the elevator. "Your name was in it."

I didn't know what rankled more—giving a *Mr.* to someone past caring about such subtleties but not to me, or the tone suggesting she and her superiors had barely begun with me.

* * *

Allen Bernstein wore a gray vest because his father and grandfather had, not because some Milan designer had ruled it a fashionable way of covering up a competitor's shirts. Sandy-haired, jowls on top of jowls, and hands borrowed from a grizzly, the lieutenant seemed to have been dropped down behind his old wooden desk and left there too long. It was even money the bottom half of his body was still mobile.

McGill stood with a foot on the radiator in the dim closet of an office as I went through my bewilderment for the third time in little more than an hour. Bernstein contributed a lot of sucking, sympathetic sounds. "Then back to square one," he said, shaking his head after I'd finished.

"Afraid so."

"Nassau Major Cases, you said? You must know Ellen Miles."

It was meant for effect, and it worked. First, I was supposed to be impressed by the conciseness of McGill's two-minute report to him before I'd been ushered into his office. Second, I had to do some uneasy shifting in my seat not to admit my resentment of Ellen Miles as one of Nassau's Finest who had declared me unwelcome in Mineola. "She was my partner for a long time. But you know that."

Bernstein was all teeth. "Sorry. An old instinct. But forget that. I'd like your input on Paz."

Input sounded like a McGill word, and Bernstein wasn't comfortable with it. But it was enough of an opening to get more for my night than reminiscences about bodies in morgues. "What do you know so far?"

He glanced at the half-smoked cigar in his ashtray as if needing its permission to lean back and encircle his head with his ham hands. Since he was already breaking the building's smoking laws, he knew what answer he was going to get. "Okay. Victor Paz arrived here early this afternoon aboard a Venezuelan freighter.

Around five o'clock he checked into a West 45th Street flophouse called the Hotel Vega. He registered with a Bolivian passport. About an hour later he was shot by an intruder in his room. We assume intruder because the deskman says nobody came calling to see him. He had about $500 in his wallet, so that seems to rule out robbery. Nobody heard the shots, and the M.E.'s naked-eye study of the slugs indicates scratches from a silencer."

"A thief could've gotten cold feet after the shooting and just run."

"Possible."

"Someone might've heard the shots but doesn't want to get involved."

"Also possible. Why rule out anything before we know what we're ruling in? But I don't think so. To any of the above."

"Why not?"

"Hold your water. I'm not finished. The only items of interest in the room were a duffel bag with clothes and a telephone address book with your name in it. Am I forgetting something, McGill?"

She seemed capable of standing with her foot on the radiator for as long as Bernstein stayed seated. "The captain of the Venezuelan ship has no idea why Paz checked into that hotel," she said. "They're sailing again to Boston the day after tomorrow."

"So we have our first theory," Bernstein sighed. "Our friend was a jumper who didn't want to see the Celtics. The clothes in his bag say he was intending to be away from the ship for more than one night."

"There's one thing that might tie it all together." I didn't know which of them I was about to contradict, but my blurt didn't leave me any room for backing out. "Drugs. He *was* robbed, but not of money. He went there for a meet. But instead of cash, he got the slugs. The clothes were for covering the drugs in his bag. And why not a silencer? He was meeting a pro."

Bernstein glanced over at McGill with such a naked show of admiration for what I'd said that I knew they had already chewed over my idea and spat it out again. "What's wrong with it?"

The fat man threw up his hands in protest. "Nothing. But I'd love it a lot more without the Bolivian passport."

"Meaning?"

"Meaning we have a mule, let's say. And he's got a rendezvous with a buyer. But the Hotel Vega? There're bars and restaurants and laundromats on every block. We've got parks and lampposts and fire hydrants on every corner. We've got *corners* on corners, for Christ sake. But not only does Paz ignore every place like that, he marches into a flophouse where he could've registered as John Smith from El Paso, but instead he slaps down this foreign passport. Like he's saying, 'Hey, pay attention, this is Victor Paz here!' That sound like a drug courier to you?"

"Maybe he was just stupid."

"Again always possible. But I like to believe the best about people, Finley. Until they show me they're morons, I assume they're Nobel Prize material, clever sons of bitches who want to make my job as unpleasant as possible. Anything else to suggest?"

I remembered why I was sitting in his stuffy office, to begin with. "What about this address book? Mine can't be the only name in it."

"Good." After a few seconds of going through a clutter of papers, he came up with a pocket-sized brown book with a thumbing index. "In fact, we have two other names, too."

Three names still didn't seem like much of an address book. "So maybe one of them gave my name to Paz."

He had trouble getting his thick thumbs into the pages. "A Rosemary Stanton from Boston. Know her?"

"No. But you said the ship was going to Boston."

"What about Hector Miranda?"

"No. Where's he from?"

Bernstein turned the book around so I could see the penciled notation of the name HECTOR MIRANDA and the number 969-8411 on an otherwise blank page. "No address, no area code. Probably a phone number, but not in Manhattan. We already checked. Might be in Bolivia."

"What about Rosemary Stanton?"

McGill finally dropped her brogan from the radiator to the floor. "She told me she met Paz in an emergency room of a hospital in La Paz a few months ago," she said. "He had a sick mother, she had a bad case of the runs. They talked a little, she had a pencil so she jotted down her address if he ever came north."

"That's all?"

"Unless she's a liar," Bernstein said. "And who's going to lie about having the runs? Anyway, that's where we are. A body pops up in this fleabag. The victim's no friend of yours, barely an acquaintance of Stanton, and who knows what to this Hector Miranda. He gets put down by what looks like a pro. His papers say he was Bolivian and a seaman. Period. I didn't even know they had water in those mountains."

"Lake Titicaca."

Bernstein's glow would have gratified the Professor; ever since the old man had given it to me as a birthday present years before, I had liked dipping into the *Columbia Encyclopedia* for facts that not even he always had at his command during his windy discourses. "That's right! That's what McGill tells me! How did you know?"

"Word gets around."

I thought I heard an uneven breath from McGill, but Bernstein thought one good crack deserved the question he had been waiting to ask since I had entered the office. "Silly to ask since you don't even know the guy, but what have you been up to today, Finley? Say between the time Paz docked and Masterson picked you up. Just for the record."

I started with the hamburgers I'd made for a late lunch, moved on to my battle with the catsup bottle, then told him about my case file on Neil Riordan. He didn't want to hear too much about Neil Riordan. "No reason to get pissed, Finley. Just do me a favor. Go home, mix yourself a drink, sit down, and start free associating. Who knows? Paz may turn out to be the son of an old lover, the brother of a friend, anything."

"I'm pretty good on names and faces. I've had to be."

He acknowledged the point with a wave of his unlighted cigar. Through a crack in the door, I could see Masterson sitting outside in the bullpen attacking a hero. At least I had discovered what he considered more pressing than Paul Finley and Victor Paz.

* * *

If you've ever had to take the **R** line from Manhattan to Bay Ridge, you know how that prospect encourages low self-esteem. The fastest part of the ride is through downtown Brooklyn, where there is a stop about every 50 yards; once past Prospect Park the motorman must keep slowing down for the new stations constantly being built along the route. Annoyed with myself for not having at least hinted to Bernstein that I wouldn't have minded being driven home, I lingered for a few minutes in front of the station house, conjuring up ideas for rounding off my big night on the town. Once I had rejected bars and bars and bars, I thought about heading down toward the East Village in search of Neil Riordan. Riordan was an old man who had gone off one morning for the proverbial pack of cigarettes, called home to say he wanted to "see New York," then dropped completely out of sight. Once I had established from his doctor that he hadn't been suffering from Alzheimer's or any other serious mental deterioration, and from his wife and friends that he was a man who "liked to do the unpredictable," I had decided Neil Riordan was a perfect challenge for Finley Investigations. If it had taken me more than 45 years to come close to spotting myself, anything less than that in catching up to old Neil promised to be a real coup for the firm.

What was good about the Riordan idea was that I would be able to charge my effort as an expense to the family and not feel like a wastrel for taking a cab home from the East Village. What was bad about it was that the temperature had dropped into the teens, and I didn't feel like walking that far even as a prelude to luxury. So, I ended up doing what I had intended doing all along: I headed west to the Hotel Vega.

No alibis: A homicide was a homicide, and not even Neil Riordan carried that kind of neon. That I'd been dragged into it by mistake, a bizarre coincidence of some kind, or—and damn, wouldn't *that* be interesting!—a devious international conspiracy was the icing on the cake. Being an innocent victim entitled me to my curiosity. There was no place to go but up, toward a stirring self-assertion pitting me against the forces of Evil.

Plus, I wasn't ready for the **R** train.

* * *

In its heyday, the Vega had probably been a welfare hotel. But a few mean twists of fate had reduced it to a shelter for ancient catatonics. There must have been a dozen of them sitting with the dirty artificial plants in the lobby—none of them under 70, most of them beyond paying attention to the snowy picture on the black-and-white portable atop a rickety table. The dread on their faces might have been for their imminent appointment with the Last Judgment or for the thought of having to trudge upstairs to their rooms for the night—or maybe that was the same thing.

The character behind the front desk had the highest ears and goofiest teeth I'd ever seen. I would have thought of him as Bugs Bunny anyway, but the sight of him chomping away at a raw carrot as he flipped through a skin magazine sealed it. Mrs. Rabbit, a potato sack with beady eyes, sat a few feet away knitting a sweater; she made me think of that French Revolution crone who got in her loops in between sending people to the guillotine.

I went straight to a lie. "Excuse me. I'm a friend of Victor Paz's."

Rabbit wasn't easily distracted by the big haunches in front of him.

"I'd like to take a look at his room."

Haunches had their limitations. So did knitted sweaters; Mrs. Rabbit eyed a new candidate for execution. "Police have sealed the room," she said.

I had anticipated that, but I also knew from my own lazy past that hotel room crime scenes were usually reopened a day or two later through nothing more than a phone call. I couldn't imagine some Yuppie prosecutor wanting to visit the Vega twice. "It'll only take a few minutes," I said, letting them both glimpse the twenty-dollar bill in my hand.

Rabbit glanced at the Missus; she was much less impressed than he was. "You a reporter?" she asked.

It was a better idea, but I stuck to mine. "Friend."

"Friends pay fifty."

"I said a few minutes, not a few hours."

Rabbit joined in enthusiastically. "Thirty-five."

In retrospect, everything might have ended right then and there. I might have taken stock of my finances realistically and gone home. But then I remembered a check I had coming from the Shea Pharmaceuticals Company for having found evidence that a former clerk hadn't been as disabled as he'd claimed because of a store fire. Catching the guy playing basketball with his sons had vindicated Shea Pharmaceuticals but hadn't done much for my Mr. Smith Goes to Washington complex. It seemed fitting I channel thirty-five of my Shea Pharmaceuticals money to the Rabbits.

Rabbit kept gnawing on his carrot as we went up the staircase and down the grungy hall of the third floor. I lighted my fourth cigarette of the day to blanket the sour odors in the air. Once I was sure the discolored linoleum wasn't going to rise up to trip me, I tried keeping my eyes off the floor. My eyes got even by making me see a capsule-sized roach trying to read the fire regulations.

At 309 Rabbit made a show of giving me the key so I would be the one responsible for breaking the police seal on the lock. He was so proud of his cleverness he rewarded himself with another chunk of carrot.

Thanks to the window that had been left open, 309 was a freezer. That was enough for Rabbit in his flannel shirt to stay at the door instead of walking in with me. The room consisted of a narrow, stained mattress with a blanket and yellow sheet balled up in the middle; a tatty bureau minus half its drawer knobs; a corner sink with a thick line of rust running between the faucets; and two spindly night tables that were far too high for the bed they were surrounding. The chalk outline showed that Paz had fallen between the bed and the window. I could make out two splotches of dried blood within the design and the work of a Crime Scene scalpel under the window sill.

"I can get you somebody." Rabbit gave me every buck tooth in his mouth. "Seventy-five dollars."

I ignored him for the ashtray on the nearer bed table. My ash was my mark on the room, I thought; now nobody can deny that I was in the room where Victor Paz was killed.

"Sixty."

"When I fall in love, I'll keep it in mind."

My mark made in the ashtray, I didn't know what else I had come for. I went over to the window mainly to feel I was getting my money's worth. The chalk confirmed my guess at the morgue that Paz had been about 5'7"; either that or the chalk man was a lousy draftsman. There was a glint in the woodwork right next to the outline. I bent down to see what it was.

"What's that? It belongs to the hotel."

It was a coin. On the front was a helmeted conquistador framed within lettering that said UN QUARTO DE BALBOA. The back was a coat-of-arms topped by an eagle that said REPUBLICA DE PANAMA.

"You find something, it belongs to the hotel."

I didn't know what Panama had to do with Bolivia or Victor Paz, but the coin felt like a better souvenir for my time than the ashes in the ashtray. I certainly had no intention of surrendering it to Rabbit, who was suddenly feeling indignant enough to brave the room's cold.

"If it's evidence, I have to give it to the cops anyway," he said.

I thought about laughing, then about knocking out some of his goofy teeth. But easiest of all was putting my hand in my coat pocket and switching the Panamanian coin with a nickel. "Here, go have a good time with it. First drink's on me."

"This nickel isn't what you picked up."

"What'd you expect—a Buffalo Head?"

"Hey, look, buddy . . ."

"I'm finished here. Thanks."

If his carrot stump had been a knife, I would have gotten it in the hand through my coat pocket. But it wasn't a knife, and Mrs. Rabbit wasn't there to back him up. "Sure this is what you picked up?"

I was feeling pretty good about that retreat until I got back downstairs and left the funereal staleness of the lobby for the night winds of the street. My overcoat had been far more effective within four walls, a floor, and a ceiling. Worse, Bernstein *did* get out from behind his desk on occasion.

"I hear you and Victor Paz have become friends."

He was holding up a blue Accord and wore nothing over his vest but his suit jacket. The cigar was going in the corner of his mouth. "It got me inside. Aren't you cold?"

"How'd you manage that without breaking the seal? You don't mean you . . .? No, even Island cops are too smart for that. That's against the law. What did you have to get inside for?"

"Maybe I just want to be ready the next time I'm asked to identify a stranger's body. Where do I get the **R** train?"

He took a moment to decide the subway threatened more torment than any he could supply over the police seal. "Get in. I'll drop you."

It wasn't like being driven all the way home, but it wasn't the moment to hold out for grand prizes. "Things that slow in the dick business?" he asked, the steering wheel looking like it was growing out of his stomach.

"You want some light on your problem, you might start with Ma and Pa Kettle in there. Anything for thirty-five bucks."

"Thirty-five! Jesus, I should switch careers!"

"I mean it. Whoever got to Paz had to get past them."

"No need to get past them at all. There's a fire escape."

I felt like an idiot for having missed that, so did my customary scrambling. "But you asked them anyway, right?"

Bernstein said nothing until he came to a red light at Broadway; the reflection from a neon sign made him look green and fretful. "Believe it or not, Finley, we have a few basic procedures here in the city, too. Maybe not up to your level, but we try."

Between the long night and his cigar's caramel sweetness, I listened to the little voice telling me to walk the rest of the way. "There's a stop at Times Square. I can walk from here."

Naturally, the light chose that moment to go green. "Here's what I found out about you, Finley," he said, slipping into the Broadway traffic. "Tell me where I miss. You stepped on the wrong toes out there in Legoland, so all the upstanding folk told you to move your shingle elsewhere. Up to then, you'd been making a passable—but only that—living chasing down malpractice butchers for an insurance company."

"That how Ellen Miles summarized it?"

"No, that's what McGill got. What I found out talking to Miles was that you were also once a pretty good cop who lost your feel for it after your wife and daughter died. She didn't come right out and say it, but I heard a little respect in her voice for you." He looked at me quickly. "I'm talking about the old, old you."

We passed the **R** station and kept going downtown. "I trained her," I said, as though that explained anything.

"Like I'm fascinated," he said, flicking an ash through his window. "Let's stick to three points. Number one, whatever happened to you out there does nothing for me one way or the other. Now that you're a city boy like us, you can enjoy the advantages of thinking of them as amateur night with too much base pay."

"Thanks."

"Point two, I really appreciated our little skull session in the office. I got a worm in here that says I'll be picking every brain the city about Paz."

"You're only hours into it!"

He tapped his nose as he rumbled over a pothole and past still another station. "I smell lamb. The kind that gets led to slaughter. Paz was *told* to go to the Vega. And whoever told him to go was waiting there to do the dirty deed or had his enemies waiting there to do it. Either way, we've got a fall guy, and that always means a smartass somewhere. I really hate smartasses, Finley. They make me work to catch up to them."

"I suppose that's point three."

He smiled. "Good for you. I'm just not a standup guy, Finley. I don't care if you used to be a cop or a bathtub. You don't tell me something I should know; I'm going to sulk."

I fingered the Panamanian coin in my pocket; it still felt like my only souvenir on the night. "Then don't sulk."

He gave me a second to change my mind, then dove straight toward the green orbs on the subway entrance at the end of the block. By the time he pulled up I had found the right wording for a question. "The freighter was heading for Boston, you said. Was New York the first stop?"

"Caracas, Vera Cruz, New York. Why?"

Vera Cruz still wasn't Panama. "I guess I'm still on my drugs theory. Maybe he also got off at Vera Cruz."

He seemed to consider it seriously. "Yeah, maybe I'm not seeing the forest for the trees. Worth checking, I guess. Thanks."

"No problem."

He leaned over to my window as I was closing the door. "Sorry I can't drive you home, but if you want a taxi, you can always send me the receipt and I can get you reimbursed."

Bernstein looked so guileless I could only shake my head. We both knew I was too close to the subway steps not to be committed to them.

TWO

Victor Paz took a back seat for a few days to an elusive husband named Morgan. Not only had Morgan abandoned his wife and three teenage daughters for a mistress, he had been countering his wife's court moves with depositions from every O'Connor and O'Malley in the city swearing she was an alcoholic who had driven Morgan out of the house and turned their daughters against him. They were right about the daughters, but not about the wife, who drank less than the magnets on my refrigerator. It turned out most of the deponents had never even met the wife, all of them worked as "board members" or "consultants" for Morgan's Fifth Avenue import-export company, and none of them showed up at the office more frequently than Morgan, who was cited going through the revolving doors about once a month. The only regulars at the 44th-floor room at 666 Fifth, in fact, were a receptionist and the mailman. Whatever the husband's company was importing and exporting, I decided, might or might not have had an IRA brand, but it reeked of the mean-spirited oafishness the Old Sod sometimes produced in the name of cleverness. I wouldn't have been surprised if a couple of my uncles showed up as Morgan's consultants.

My second semester at the university started well with a class on community statutes versus municipal laws. One of the kids taught me a few extra twists of the screw with stories about the Kew Gardens coop where she lived with her parents. Having been enlightened once on the evening, I decided to double my winnings by dropping in on the Professor. I walked into a mob scene. Instead of the usual soiree with Pinot Grigio on the table, the coffee table was sagging under scotch, bourbon, gin, and vodka. There had to be 25 or 30 people spread out over the living room, kitchen, and long hall between them, and they were doing a lot more He-Said She-Said than listening to the Professor's latest views on the Punic Wars. The party turned out to be for celebrating the engagement of two of the Professor's protégés.

Of course, Phil and Barbara Ortega were there. The most interesting new face belonged to Angela Balestrini, a visiting researcher from Buenos Aires who was staying with them in Sea Cliff. It took Angela Balestrini all of ten seconds to make it clear she wasn't as impressed by policemen past or present as Ortega was, and did us both a favor by smiling off his invitation to ask me about the Time That. Somewhere in the middle of all this dancing around Victor Paz popped out.

"I never knew there were Bolivian sailors," somebody said. "Isn't the country landlocked?"

"There is Lake Titicaca," Angela said delicately. "They have a coast guard and do a lot of shipping."

Cross-legged on the floor in front of the couch, Ortega burped a laugh. "They also have feet. And sometimes they use them to go to a railway station or an airport and wind up in Chile or Venezuela or some other place where ships are hiring. That makes them Bolivian seamen, too, doesn't it?"

It was such an obvious point I was dismayed it hadn't come up with Bernstein. It wasn't that we had overlooked something exactly, but Ortega's observation made me feel I'd been hasty about Paz in some important way.

Because of Paz Angela Balestrini decided I had more to offer than remembrances of past felonies. I extended my cultural horizons by quizzing her about the Italian community in Argentina, learning along the way that there were more Italians in Buenos Aires than in Rome and that she had a sense of humor. All the while Ortega was sinking to the bottom of the scotch bottle he had appropriated as his own. Mention of Paz had spurred him into talking about his vacation in Colombia, then into reviewing a career that he worried offered more financial and social rewards than spiritual satisfactions. It was self-pity of the worst academic sort, and I had to look away every time he raised a fish-mouthed smile at me from the floor, silently beseeching me to find the sincerity behind his frameless glasses.

I suppose I should have looked for it. The guy had been nothing but friendly toward me. I even admired how he wanted. That's right, *wanted*. Whatever else he was, Phil Ortega was no natural heir to the tweeds and pipes of a faculty room. A couple of years older than I was, he had the look of somebody who had worked at maintaining the tight, wiry frame of a middleweight boxer. His body said he had never gotten anything easily. Even in his fawning over me, I'd sensed he was evening some old score with grayheads who had once told him it couldn't be done—that an ex-cop in a classroom couldn't be done and that Phil Ortega, successful academic, couldn't be done. Whoever the grayheads had been he still liked showing them they were wrong.

And hated himself for turning into the academic bum of the month.

"You like thinking what you're doing is good, is necessary," he moaned after most of the company had left. "That just one Indio might live more humanly because I helped persuade Generalissimo Butcher he has to rotate crops or import light machinery or decentralize his administration. But what happens? The Generalissimo's flacks go, 'Fabulous, Ortega,' they give me a splendid dinner at the best restaurant in the city, then a big airport send-off. The next I hear about any of it is some *Nation* column where I'm being called a fascist or a CIA agent. I don't think that's fair."

"The people who write for that kind of magazine don't understand anything," Barbara Ortega volunteered through an awkward silence.

"Some do, Barbara. Some do."

Barbara hesitated again, waiting for somebody else to beat her to the reassurances. But Angela tried to look distracted with a book she had taken off the Professor's shelf, the Professor seemed to have too much to say to know where to start, and I had my own scotch to think about. "Well, who are you supposed to be giving advice to?" she finally said. "A couple of rebels in the bush?"

That was too crude for Ortega. "You're not listening, Barbara. I *know* the Generalissimo's a butcher. Nobody's forcing me to be a sounding board for him. I can't rationalize it away so easily. I'm Latino, too."

When she wasn't looking glum, Barbara Ortega was on the verge of huffing and puffing. She hadn't wanted one of their private conversations played out before an audience, but now that it was in the open she was ready to take on the riffraff responsible for putting doubts in her husband's head. I didn't like being told I was riffraff. "So what's your point, Phil?" I asked, hoping to head her off.

"My point."

"You have one, don't you?"

No, he didn't; but he could drink to that, too. "What else but my little Indio?" he smiled, raising his glass. "My one and only little Indio."

"What about him?"

He leaned over to slap me on the knee. "You know as well as I do, Finley. All the hypocrisy that fucker's responsible for. Am I right?"

Why disagree if it shut him up?

"Sad pair," the Professor pronounced after the Ortegas and Angela had left. "She's stupid and he's got no balls."

"Sure of that, are you?"

He pushed all the empty bottles together on the table, looked over his achievement, then decided that was as much as he was going to do before going to bed. "You hear something I didn't?"

"I'm being nice to weaklings this week. Maybe it's self-interest."

Joe Carroll wasn't amused. "I don't like my weaklings advising governments," he snapped. "The wrong people always get the sand kicked in their faces. So, you going home or staying here tonight?"

I considered my answer a sign of growing mental health. The same question a short time before would have had me dwelling on the last time I'd slept off a dizzy head at the Professor's and running out the door. But that night his couch had the last word and nobody got killed because of it.

The killing came 24 hours later.

* * *

At home the next day I tried ignoring my hangover by doubling back on all the character witnesses my Irish friend Morgan had disinterred for declaring his wife an unfit mother. As I mentioned, most of them were tied to the curious Fifth Avenue company that did such lousy business nobody bothered to show up for work. One of them was not, however. Looking closer at the depositions Mrs. Morgan's lawyer had given me, I came across a Patrick Hardy. There was no Hardy on Morgan's stationery or in the tax papers filed for the import-export company. Was Patrick Hardy the Achilles heel in Morgan's forces? Why include him with the other slanderers?

Queens Information gave me Hardy's number at the Woodside address on the deposition. Hardy didn't answer on the third or fourth ring. By the fifth ring, I was more interested in my own handwriting, staring up at me from my notepad and shouting out HARDY, WOODSIDE, 969-7345. The 969 was the same prefix I'd read for Hector Miranda when Bernstein had shown me Victor Paz's address book. 969 wasn't a Manhattan prefix, but it could have been a Queens one!

I put down the receiver before Patrick Hardy did or didn't pick up. Proud of my memory for the 969-8411 that had come back to me from Paz's page, I tapped out the number. I didn't know what to expect as an answer, but I wondered again if Bernstein hadn't been a little too cavalier about dismissing the drugs possibility. I liked the idea I was calling some public phone in the Little Bogota section of Jackson Heights.

"*Sí?*"

"Hector Miranda?"

Hesitation. "*Sí.*"

I pictured Bernstein and McGill sitting on my couch and looking chagrined. "Mr. Miranda, I'm a friend of Victor Paz."

"Who?" No hesitation.

"Victor Paz? From Bolivia?"

Someone was banging pots and pans behind Miranda. It wasn't a pay phone on Roosevelt Avenue, I told myself, it was the lab itself, and I had interrupted a distilling session. "You have the wrong number, Mister. I don't know this Victor Paz."

Why did I believe him right away? Probably because I'd had the same reaction when Masterson had come calling. "Mr. Miranda, this is hard to explain," I started babbling, "but your name was given to me . . . well, sort of through a Victor Paz."

He laughed. "That's good. You need car service?"

"You drive a cab?"

"What do you need—taxi? Limousine?"

Had Hector Miranda's name ended up in Paz's book because he had driven him from the waterfront to the Hotel Vega? It didn't seem likely, but then either did Rosemary Stanton's connection to the dead man. "Tell you what, Mr. Miranda. I'm going to be out in your neighborhood later today. Maybe we can work out something."

"Sure. What time?"

I spent the next couple of minutes trying to sound like a would-be customer and getting his address. When I hung up, I didn't have the slightest idea of what I had accomplished except to have tracked down the third person in the address book to Jackson Heights. It wasn't much, but it was more than Bernstein and McGill had done, and that seemed to entitle me to more than just calling the fat man and crowing about my superior enterprise. Plus, there was the serendipity factor: Patrick Hardy lived in Woodside, only a few blocks from Miranda. Why not kill two birds with one drive and have the whole city cheering me from the rooftops?

* * *

It was a little after seven when I arrived in Woodside. Most of the commuters were long home, even some of the supermarkets were starting to close, and the #7 El was running over Roosevelt Avenue between fairly long stretches. I assumed one of the commuters home was Patrick Hardy, but since he hadn't answered my calls over the afternoon, I gave him a few more minutes by heading first for Miranda's address. Two blocks shy of 61st Street, a cop was standing in the middle of Roosevelt Avenue and furiously waving all traffic east.

It took me ten minutes to find a parking space on a side block of three-family houses and another ten minutes to get back to where cars and buses were being detoured. Police lines had been set up on the other side of Roosevelt, and there was a caravan of ambulances, squad cars, and unmarked police vehicles parked zigzag behind the barrier. EMS attendants were running from the rubble with stretchers and oxygen apparatus. The air stank with smoke. Getting as close to the barrier as I could, I counted the address numbers down to the rubble and then past it. The address Hector Miranda had given me was the ruin in between.

Two teenagers in sweatshirts advertising a salsa show jostled past me for a better look. They could have slugged me and I wouldn't have felt it. There was serendipity and there was fear, but I had never thought of them as the same thing before. The kids were impressed; they had never seen the effects of a bomb blast before. An elderly Hispanic next to me blessed himself at the sight of another EMS team emerging from the twisted metal and heaped bricks. He had a point: The body inside the bag being hauled off by the paramedics was either only pieces of a body or a child. I lighted a cigarette as the murmuring rose around me. I felt like following my match into the sewer grating.

Then I saw a familiar face. Frank Vincent was hurrying up from the rubble, wiping his hand over his bristly crewcut as he came. That was more emotion than I was used to seeing from Vincent. As a member of the federal prosecutor's office, he had been in on the last act of the homicide case that had earned me a leper's status in Nassau County. I'd heard he had made a lateral career move to the FBI since then. He had done his job on the homicide, but he hadn't liked me for helping to make it necessary.

I was still debating about whether to call out to him when he stopped at the unmarked car closest to the barrier, started to reach through his window for his radio, then spotted me. He blinked to be sure, and I told myself his ashy color had been caused by the blast site, not by me.

"You have a reason for being here, Finley?"

The icy question brought me immediate interest from the teenagers. My little voice said not to be smart. "The crowd. How's it going, Frank?"

He seemed stymied for a second, then motioned for the cop at the barrier to pass me through. It didn't feel like a privilege. I was suddenly in the wrong kind of math. Victor Paz had been a foreign national with a passport, so Bernstein had to have informed the Feds about the address book. I could even imagine that Vincent had been about to put in a radio call about me and the Stanton woman in Boston.

Up close Vincent was still the pouty-faced ex-Marine with the Juicy Fruit breath who hadn't liked me for turning against Ellen Miles and the Nassau cops. "Let's do it again. Why are you here?"

"Hector Miranda. I had an appointment with him."

He had been expecting everything but the truth. "About what?"

The EMS ambulance hit its siren as it pulled out; I didn't understand the hurry. "The book you heard about. I don't like mysteries."

He didn't miss his opening. "Right. You're a dedicated problem solver. Okay, so why don't we go down to my office and talk . . .?"

I saw McGill first—same bomber jacket, corduroys, and klutzy brogans. She was sitting on the stoop of the house next to the bombed out one and talking to a woman wrapped in a blanket.

"You listening, Finley?"

Vincent already had his back door opened. Bernstein and McGill suddenly looked better. "There's nothing I can tell you, Frank, except I talked to the guy today and made an appointment to see him tonight. I figured if I knew why his name was in Paz's address book, I might also figure out why mine was."

"So we'll explore that together. Come on. Get in."

Call me kvetchy. It had been only a few days since I'd jumped up on Masterson's lap and ended up stranded in Manhattan; I had no intention of being driven to another midtown office and then being told I was free to return to Queens to retrieve my car. "You have sufficient cause, Frank, I want to hear it. Otherwise, I'm going nowhere."

"Sufficient cause!"

"You're in charge of this investigation, that right?"

Surprisingly, it was a bulls-eye. "You know better than that," he said, but more weakly.

In his place, I would have come up with ten better answers, including the most obvious one that I was pretty material where witnesses were concerned. But then Bernstein made everything academic.

"Well, well. Here you're in my thoughts and here you are in person!"

Seeing the fat man made me feel like a puppy relieved to see his master after a long absence. "You still running things, Lieutenant, or is he?"

Neither of them appreciated my big mouth, but as long as I had asked, Bernstein also looked interested in the answer. Vincent suddenly had another appointment. "Let's make it tomorrow at ten, Bernie," he said, slamming his back door closed. "Your office. You can send me the paperwork from here tonight, and we'll all be up to speed."

Bernstein conceded a nod.

"And if I were you, I'd keep my hands on our friend here."

Vincent didn't wait for Bernstein's reaction, getting behind the wheel and lurching off toward the barrier at the far end of the street. "He doesn't seem to like you," Bernstein said drily.

"I remind him of unpleasant things."

"Try not to have the same effect on me."

I didn't dare jerk him around. I told him everything, from my phone conversation with Miranda to my intention of calling on Patrick Hardy. It might have sounded more candid if, in the middle of my rundown, the woman in the blanket with McGill hadn't suddenly grasped what she had lost and shattered the street with a shriek from Hell. Bernstein winced as he watched an EMS worker break through a circle of neighbors to get to the woman. "Looks like seven, maybe eight victims," he said. "The Mirandas on the ground floor, a cousin and his family on the other two. Two kids, maybe three. A very professional device attached to the heater."

It took me a second to see what he was getting at. "He was a gypsy cabbie! What's that got to do with me?"

He trained his skepticism on the cigar he was unwrapping. "A gypsy cabbie, a merchant seaman. *Some*body's drawing a line and connecting the dots. Why not a private dick next?"

It was crazy as a theory, but not as a feeling. "I never heard of either one of them. Why can't you get that through your head?"

"Miranda was absolutely sure he'd never met Paz?"

"The guy was looking for a fare. I had an idea . . ."

"What?"

"Well, maybe he picked up Paz and brought him to the hotel."

Bernstein thought about it, took out his Bic, and made a note. "I don't imagine we'll ever know now."

The thought of a hit list with my name on it settled more deeply into my nerves. "We'll never know because you and your dynamite team from the big city can't be bothered to dial a 718 area code!"

"Easy does it. We're just talking."

"And they're just being carted off down there."

He gazed down at the ruined house, where McGill was now talking to a Latin in a brown mackinaw. "Suppose I give you a fact, Finley?" he asked, lighting his cigar. "Give me one back?"

"If I can."

He wanted more but accepted what he had. "Forget about drugs and money and sex. What do politics say to you?"

Vincent was the FBI, I reminded myself. "Nothing."

"Nothing you're working on right now involves political types?"

"Not really."

"Then unreally."

I started telling him my fantasies about Morgan and the Irish color to the divorce and custody case. He wasn't enthusiastic, and shouldn't have been: Once I was articulating my suspicions about the import-export company, they seemed like so much dishwater.

"I mean Latin American politics. Anything in that area?"

"No."

He blew a smoke ring. He believed me and didn't want to.

"What did Vincent tell you?"

"Need to know."

"You're hinting *I* need to know to cover my ass."

"Yeah. And you may not be able to cover it. You might really need your buddy Vincent's protection."

"No, thanks."

He started slowly back down the block, taking it for granted I would trail along. The cigar got weaker and weaker the closer we got to the rubble's thick, acrid smell. "According to Vincent," he said finally, "Paz was not a fan of his government. He didn't think too much of the Bolivian ambassador to the UN, either."

I said nothing; there were millions of words in the English language I was afraid would cut off his confidence, and I didn't want to risk using any of them. Close enough to her now, I could hear McGill speaking to the Latin in the Mackinaw. Her Spanish didn't sound like something she had picked up from language records.

"Paz was no sailor," he said. "The Feds red-flagged him weeks ago. He was coming to tell the ambassador personally what he thought of him."

"A hitman?"

"A believer. Vincent thinks embassy security got to him first."

"That's nuts."

"Think so? I'll tell you something even nuttier. Vincent's people have a bee in their bonnet those people in the address book were Paz's contacts here. What do you make of that?"

I thought of my conversation with the cabbie Hector Miranda, then of the dysentery story about Rosemary Stanton. By the time I got back to thinking about me, Frank Vincent and I were standing on different planets in the solar system.

"That's what I figured," Bernstein said.

"Don't tell me you believe that crap!"

He stared at the remains of a spice shelf that had been blown to the edge of the sidewalk; the backboard had been splintered after the letters CINNAM. "Not much. But then I look at this and I also know we're not talking about some fare who got into a snit because Miranda took the long way in from the airport. Help me out, Finley. There's something in that skull of yours I need to know."

Maybe it was the appeal of his tired eyes. Maybe it was remembering how I'd felt sometimes when I was convinced somebody wasn't cooperating as much as he could have. Maybe it was even thinking again about how Phil Ortega had thrown out that other obvious definition of a Bolivian seaman. Whatever the reason, I was suddenly sure my name had not been in Paz's book by mistake, that I *had* overlooked something.

Then I realized what somebody else had overlooked. "Vincent wasn't very insistent, was he?"

"About what?"

"What you just told me. If he's got all this pegged so neatly, why am I standing here with you instead of in his car going back to his office?"

McGill came over before Bernstein could answer. With me there she needed his nod before reporting what she had learned from the man in the Mackinaw and others. "I got four people identifying a Con Ed truck here about four o'clock. Two men, probably Latino, told Mrs. Miranda they had to go to the basement to check on a line. She let them in."

"License?"

She shrugged. "Who looks at a utility truck's plates?"

They went through the numbers. Calls would be made to Con Edison. Composite sketches of the suspects would be made. One of the Miranda cousins, who appeared likely to survive, would have a guard posted outside his room at Booth Memorial. The Crime Scene people would drop everything else until they had completed a preliminary report.

I began to feel like a fifth wheel. And hated myself for even thinking maybe I would be better off as one—safely stowed away in some trunk until everything had been cleared up.

* * *

When I got back to my neighborhood, I was more in the mood for the Green Fox than my living room. I took a stool at the short arm as Cynthia nodded to me from the end of the bar, then went back to slicing oranges and lemons. She was still working on returning me to the status of just another customer and still doing it wrong. Even just another customer, I snarled to myself, wouldn't put up with being kept waiting so long to order.

I put up with it. The only regulars there were Rachel and Johnny Yeager, in the middle of one of their philosophical discussions on What Was Wrong With (fill in the blank) Nowadays. I thought about sarcastically asking them their opinion of the latest internal political developments in Bolivia, then remembered they might have a more learned one than I had.

Cynthia finally had enough lemon and orange slices for the mysterious fruit salad crowd she was expecting and ambled down to me. Her blonde curls were pushed too far back from her forehead, exactly the way I'd once told her I didn't like them. "The usual?"

I thought about saying, no, I'd have her latest Mongolian beer with a creme de menthe chaser, but my nerves weren't up for it. It had only hit me in the car driving back: Vincent might *not* have been wrong. At that very moment gunsels from the Bolivian legation to the UN might have been prowling the streets for me in the belief I wanted to do in their ambassador. What the hell was I paying taxes for? Didn't that entitle me to some protection from foreign gunmen?

"You see a ghost?"

Cynthia laid my scotch in front of me. She was wearing the same denim shirt and skirt as she had the first night I'd gone upstairs with her to her apartment. I didn't like the small rush that came with the reminder: It felt too much like a doomed man recalling the highlights of his life.

"I found another name in that messy custody case I was telling you about. Maybe it's this Morgan's weak link."

She had been expecting more. "So that's good, right?"

"Maybe."

"Still think it's the IRA?"

I thought about smothering everyone I had ever shared that demented theory with. "Yeah. They're not satisfied throwing the Brits out of Belfast, they want Mrs. Morgan out of her house, too."

She gave me one of her best raspy laughs. It sounded so instinctive I remembered people did have instincts and that I must have just misplaced mine in some drawer of my bureau.

THREE

I picked the wrong evening to bother Phil Ortega with questions about Bolivia. I found him in his office inspecting his dinner jacket in a mirror. "You should read the trees and bulletin boards around here, my friend. We don't get the Commerce Secretary to dinner every night. I bet you didn't hear his speech this afternoon, either."

"Sorry."

He threw up his arms theatrically, then hurried around behind his desk to gather up his wallet, keys, and scraps of paper he'd left there. "Okay, you're not impressed. What is it—a class problem?"

The *Times* sat on a corner of his desk. Unless it was a special private edition, it said what mine had said that morning: that the Jackson Heights explosion three days before had "probably" been caused by some central heater "malfunction," that seven people were still dead, and that the investigation continued. "I'm looking for a book on Bolivian politics. Something that goes a little deeper than what United Fruit likes."

Ortega smiled. "Some people say that's as deep as it gets. What's this for—one of your cases?"

I'd made up my mind not to go into detail with him. It had taken me three days to consign Vincent's fantasies to a harmless place and I didn't want to give anyone a chance to summon them up again. "Yeah, one of my clients is from there."

He jabbed his thumb at the bookcase that covered his broadest wall from floor to ceiling. "They're in alphabetical order, which means Bolivia's up on the top. Start with the ones laying down. That means they're new and I haven't read them yet. What's the case?"

"Just an inheritance claim. What government was in office when, so what government owes what."

"Oh, boy, you may have a doozy on your hands! One general alone has been in and out office three times."

"Great. The messier it is, the more per diems I collect." I had expected a laugh, but he looked annoyed. "I say something?"

Ortega took a moment to shake his head and get back to stuffing his pockets. "I guess I'm getting touchier in my old age. That way you put it about the messiness has been the attitude of these tin soldiers the State Department has put in power, too . . . Never mind. You just hit my unfunny bone. Look, I've got to run. Take what you need. Just leave me a note what it is. And turn off the lights after you, okay?"

"Sure. Have a good dinner."

"Learn the lingo, Finley. You don't have 'good' dinners with a Commerce Secretary. They're 'informative' and 'profitable.' See you."

I waited until I couldn't hear him in the hall, then pulled a desk chair over to the bookcase and got up on it to reach the top shelf. There were three books laid horizontally in the Bolivian section. Two were in Spanish and seemed to be cultural histories of some kind. I almost toppled off the chair when I read the cover of the third one as BOLIVIA ABOVE GROUND BY PHILIP ORTEGA.

I got back down to the floor before I let any thought in. Per the flyleaf, BOLIVIA ABOVE GROUND was "an original look at a unique Latin nation long associated only with its mining industry . . . but in fact, variegated . . . diversified . . . kaleidoscope." Ortega himself was "one of the most astute and observant . . . scholar . . . expert . . . authority."

I stared over at what appeared to be a wooden flute dangling off one of the high shelves. I thought of a record of Andes Indian songs Jennifer had once bought. I thought of llamas and old Indios wearing fedoras. And then I thought I didn't give a damn if

BOLIVIA ABOVE GROUND turned out to be about Andes clouds, I didn't like Ortega's false modesty.

The nice thing about being peevish, of course, is that you can keep milking it until you've blamed one person for your nonexistent bank account, your lousy love life, and the Middle East crisis. As I glared at the book in my hand, I told myself there was more than coincidence in meeting Phil Ortega and then soon after popping up in the address book of a Bolivian assassin. How many countries in the world were there? Almost three hundred? And suddenly the same one-three-hundredth of that equation showed up in two different places within months of each other? If I believed in that kind of luck, I would have done nothing but play the state lottery.

I might have sat there churning myself to a ridiculous boil until class if Angela Balestrini hadn't stuck her head in the door. She was as startled to see me in any form as I was to see her in a black formal with spaghetti straps and with her hair pushed up into a small bun. Twenty feet away from her I could smell the Chanel.

"No, I haven't taken over. Phil just left."

"Oh. Barbara and I were going to pick him up for the dinner."

"Yeah, well."

She fidgeted, and I blamed myself for not preventing it with better conversation. Her face was narrow enough not to turn applish because of the bun; maybe it was just her heels and the black dress and stockings, but I hadn't remembered her being so tall at the Professor's.

"You're not attending?"

"No, I have a class. Plus, nobody invited me."

"Well, I don't think you're going to miss very much. These official dinners are always so . . ."

"Official?"

"Exactly. Barbara and I are going to support each other."

I didn't believe that about Barbara Ortega, but I wanted to believe it about Angela Balestrini. I also wanted to believe she represented serendipity after finding BOLIVIA ABOVE GROUND. "Have you read this?"

I held the book up as if giving her eye test. She squinted, then thought better of it and let go of the door handle to walk in a few steps. "Oh, Phil's! No, I'm embarrassed to say I haven't yet."

I threw the dice. "Probably very academic, huh? Not what you'd need for an introduction to Bolivia."

"That depends on what you want to be introduced to."

"Right."

"Are you asking something in particular? Barbara *is* waiting."

I hadn't been throwing the dice before, I realized; *now* I was. "I just can't figure out Ortega. You heard him when he gets some scotch in him. But then he gets . . . very official."

It didn't sound all that unique put that way, but she tried to be nice about it. "That's a complex question. Intellectuals have their ideas, academics their practical calculations. We could talk about it sometime. But I really should be going now."

I would have given myself a full 100 points in jerkdom is she hadn't paused halfway out the door with the reminder that she could be reached at the Ortegas' place—"better in the early morning."

I waited until Angela's heels had faded down the hall before making a note to Ortega I'd taken his book, turning off the desk lamp, and leaving. Since I was still a half-hour early for class, I cut through the parking lot for a coffee in the cafeteria. A bitter wind had picked up since I'd driven in, so I stopped off at my car for the sweater I had in the back. While pulling the sweater over my head, I conducted another of my periodic surveys on the affluence of the student body. Even the three cars that were older than my Saturn looked newer. I was glad to see my teaching salary remained demographically appropriate.

I was about ten feet away from my car, starting to stoke bright notions about Angela Balestrini when the gravel behind me kicked up too noisily. I was still turning when the ferret I kept as a secret pet jumped on my nerves. It took a bite, there was more splattered gravel, and the engine that should have stopped humming so near me didn't. I wasted a fraction of a second trying to pick up a piece of chrome between the glaring lights, then finally moved whatever remained of my body to dive for the tail of a black

DeVille. The DeVille's fender came up to meet my forehead half-way but then shied off, leaving my hands and balls to the gravel. I wasted another few lives picturing the exhaust pipe poking out my eye, only after that realizing I still had both ankles as the car shot past toward the exit. By the time I looked around all I could make out was that it was a dark Toyota with only the driver. He hit the boulevard as if he had more targets in mind.

Somebody opened a window in the dorm building over the lot and shouted. I didn't know if he was shouting at me or the Toyota. I didn't need his indignation. The pebbles embedded in my palms felt angry enough.

* * *

The Professor's therapy consisted of one part iodine and Band-Aids, one part scotch, and one part telephone. He didn't want to hear about how I'd gotten through my class with my hands wrapped in handkerchiefs; the one and only thing he wanted to hear was me talking on the kitchen phone to Bernstein. "You call him or I will."

"You're imagining things, Joe."

"What the hell am I imagining? That guy in the hotel room? Those people blown all over Queens? What's this cop's number?"

Like Julius Caesar, I had put up enough empty protests before the sight of him weighing the kitchen receiver like a club. Or had I just needed to hear his fear matching my own? "Okay, give me the damn thing."

Easier said than done. You should close your hand to grip a receiver, and my Band-Aids needed some drilling on that exercise. Worse, you have to talk to someone like Bernstein sounding like a paranoid or a frightened citizen in need of police protection. I didn't think I was the former and I didn't want the latter.

The fat man seemed to understand. "Okay. What about to-night—you staying at your father-in-law's?"

Why make things easy? "No, I'm going home right now."

"Not for an hour you're not. And drive very, very slowly. I want your apartment checked out. Of course, if they kamikaze you on the LIE there's nothing I can do about it."

"That's funny."

"I thought so."

"What about Miranda? Anything I should know?"

His sigh was decidedly peevish. "We got this a little backward, don't we, Finley? It's what I should know."

Ortega's book sat on the kitchen counter in front of me, looking like an extra sock from the washing machine. "I'm working on a thought."

"How nice for you."

"If it was anything concrete, I'd tell you."

"Then you work on making it concrete and let me get Masterson in here. Remember, at least an hour."

"Right . . . Bernstein?"

"Yeah?"

"Assuming just for the sake of argument . . ."

"The Stanton woman? My next call. Anything else, chief?"

"No, I guess you're on top of things."

"Appreciate your confidence."

I clapped down the receiver and listened to the noise fill up the kitchen. Whatever the Professor was doing in the living room, he was doing it in absolute silence. I grabbed the book from the counter and brought it inside to him. He was in his lounger, staring down at the rug and twiddling his thumbs over the paunch that had almost doubled since he had begun his soirees. He had already set the book aside brusquely in the kitchen and didn't like getting it thrown at him again. "I don't read books with graphs on every goddamn page."

"Historians never stoop to that, huh?"

"Not ones I admire." He picked the book off his lap reluctantly. "What am I looking for?"

"A connection between Paz and Ortega."

"Where? In all these numbers about copper and sugar?"

"There's got to be a connection, Joe."

"Just because they're both from Latin America?"

"He could've told me he'd written that book."

"Oh, yeah, there's a smoking gun."

"Then just call it my gut."

He chewed on that, then came up out of the book with the kind of troubled look I'd seen only when he contemplated the photo of Jennifer and Susan atop the TV set. "When you were involved with all those big bullshitters out here," he said, "I could see you were in over your head. But you survived, even came out a little better for it. But this stuff scares me more. At least you *knew* why you were up against that Mineola scum."

"So what am I supposed to do? Rent a cell next to Bernstein's office? We tried that kind of living once, Joe."

His face reddened so fast I became alarmed. Then he suddenly fired the book at the couch. "I should've never brought you back out here!"

I was astonished. "Is that what all this fussing's about? You blame yourself for introducing me to Ortega?"

"Well, it's sure a helluva coincidence, isn't it?"

It sounded completely different coming from somebody else, and I wasn't ready for it. "We're just guessing."

"Right," he said tartly. "New world. Strike up Dvorak. Once upon a time somebody like Ortega would have sat there on the rug talking about the masses revolting, gotten you to agree, then run off to the FBI to report you as a Commie agent. Nowadays they don't have to do that. They're in and out of so many government grants and corporation boards they've become their own FBI agents. But it's the same entrapment. They need alibis for their lack of balls and that means dragging others down with them."

My little voice told me not to debate the point, that I was on the receiving end of more than some variation on his guilt about Jennifer and Susan. "Then find that out for me," I answered. "Find me a handle. We'll give it to Bernstein and then go skiing until they sort out all the bad guys."

His laugh came out as a snort. "Skiing!"

"Or we'll go to a movie."

He nodded, then pulled himself up from the lounger to retrieve BOLIVIA ABOVE GROUND. It was hardly a revelation, but it hit me as I watched him lumber over to the couch that he was the only family I had left.

* * *

I got home just as Masterson was coming out of the building. He told me two bomb squad people had been through every drawer in my apartment and had moved downstairs for a look at the boiler room. "Of course this setup isn't like Jackson Heights," he said, appraising the five floors of windows above us. "Blow this place and you got another Pearl Harbor. Anyway, the locals will keep an eye on you tonight."

A peek into my garbage upstairs told me the bomb people preferred Pepsi to Bud Lite. I took my remaining can of soda for supper and went to my desk. Why fret about all the faceless people who want to kill you when you can work out a schedule for the next day? And I certainly had enough things to schedule. I still hadn't interviewed Patrick Hardy in Woodside for the Morgan divorce case. I still hadn't checked out a Catholic hospice in Canarsie that the missing Neil Riordan had apparently once praised to his wife as someplace he wouldn't mind living in. And I'd also been putting off a look at whether a deadbeat who had stiffed Mrs. Morgan's lawyer on a separate matter had truly abandoned his apartment without leaving a forwarding address. But a few minutes into lining up my ducks for the next day I was back to thinking about my ripped-up hand and practicing a few reaches into my pocket to see if I could finger coins without clutching at flames. As a domestic sport, it wasn't all that exciting; on the other hand, it reminded me that Balboa had discovered the Pacific Ocean.

I threw the Panamanian coin down on the file containing Martin Lucchese's deadbeat deeds with Mrs. Morgan's lawyer. I told myself I still owed it to Bernstein to tell him where I'd found it, but I'd had the identical thought every time I'd pulled it out of my pocket looking for change. I didn't really believe the coin was important, but it nagged me as a small act of bad faith toward the fat man.

Then Balboa discovered something more significant than the Pacific. He was sitting right below the biographical sketch the lawyer had given me of Martin Lucchese. Lucchese had been an ungrateful son of a bitch. Thanks to my lawyer-employer, he had won a case against his landlord about undone repairs in his Cobble Hill apartment. But when the lawyer's $2650 bill had come due, Lucchese had first hemmed and hawed, and then had either sublet the apartment and skipped town or taken to disguising his voice on the phone with the sublet story. The lawyer had hardly gone into bankruptcy without his $2650, but he'd asked me to check out Lucchese as a chaser to the Morgan affair. What I hadn't noticed in Lucchese's bio before Balboa had pointed it out to me was that Martin came from Boston.

I don't believe in horoscopes, but I read mine in the *News* every day. I don't believe in Ouija boards, either, but the sight of the Panamanian coin atop the word Boston struck me as the next best thing to a gust of wind coming through the window and a disembodied voice croaking FINLEY! FINLEY! WHY HAVE YOU LET ME DIE? From there it was easy persuading myself I'd find out something from Rosemary Stanton she had been reluctant to share with the cops. As a fellow victim in the Victor Paz Riddle, wouldn't I be more likely than a cop to recognize a pertinent detail? And while I was in Boston, I could call up one of the ten thousand Martin Luccheses listed in the phone book and demand $2650.

I didn't think I was being whimsical. Before nodding off that night I promised myself I'd forget the whole thing if I woke up less convinced by the idea. That commitment was good for picturing the Professor, Bernstein, and McGill taking turns at reproaching me for my capricious ways. They were still going at it hot and heavy when I finally fell off.

* * *

There's too much Connecticut and Rhode Island between New York and Boston—enough to make anyone have second thoughts about the drive. Lucky for my sense of resolve, I'd gotten the numbers of the four Rosemary Stantons listed by Boston Information before leaving the house and had hit the right one on the second call. She had come across as a husky-throated 40ish altogether dubious about being bothered by another call about somebody she had barely known. But since I was going to be in Boston anyway as part of the global manhunt for Martin Lucchese, I was able to prevail on her to make a few minutes for me.

Thanks to her precise instructions, I came upon the Back Bay pub off Cambria Street with little trouble. I parked on a cobblestoned side street that existed only for a musical instruments store midway along and a four-story garage at the end of the cul-de-sac. I read every sign three times before I was satisfied my car wouldn't be towed, then went into the corner pub called the Wooden Quarter. I liked the omen of the coin motif.

My telephone picture hadn't been far off. Sitting in a window booth with a daiquiri before her, Rosemary Stanton was a smartly suited palomino blonde in her late thirties or early forties. Her dark brown eyes said she didn't suffer fools easily, but there was a softness to her chin that left her mouth open in a perpetual surprise.

Over my beer, I told her how Masterson had introduced me to Victor Paz and how I'd run down every Dominican shortstop I'd ever heard of without producing a connection between me and Latin America. I left out Ortega as too flimsy speculation. I also left out the explosion part of Hector Miranda when her bemusement at my tale told me she hadn't heard about it. I finished embroidering my story, ordered a second beer, and listened to how she'd met Paz in the Bolivian emergency room during a vacation in La Paz. What I still did not hear after more than a half-hour of back and forth was a single word about Boston's Finest visiting her to offer her protection. I didn't like that missing piece at all. Was she being more evasive than she appeared or had Bernstein run into some Boston clod who thought of New York's problems as New York's problems?

"There isn't much more to tell," she said. "I went chattering on about Boston to keep my mind off my stomach, and Victor kept looking over at the door expecting the doctor to walk in any second with bad news about his mother. I just gave him my address. It seemed like the thing to do."

"Did his mother make it?"

She smiled shrewdly. "That's what Sergeant McGill asked, and with the same shifty tone. No, Mr. Finley, I didn't see Victor Paz after that night in the hospital so I have no idea about his mother."

"Sorry."

"I wouldn't have minded. Four weeks in the Andes, and he was the only person I talked to outside hotel clerks and the other members of my tour group. But at the time I was preoccupied with my unladylike ailment." I nodded; *lady* was right for her. "And no idea about who killed him?"

Frank Vincent and his assassination plots felt much further away than New York. "Just a lot of guessing."

"I have a theory," she said, suddenly playful.

"What's that?"

"Speaking as an expert on telephone address books," she said. "Every New Year's Eve I convene a little courtroom here in my head to decide who deserves to be in that year's edition. This one goes because she's a bore. He can stay because he's been a true friend."

"A new book every year?"

"It's a present I give myself," she said, finishing her drink. "What it really is, of course, is a merit review of the people I know. Making myself look at them the way I don't otherwise. I'm the judge, queen, giver of graces, and executioner."

"Heavy load. How do you read Paz?"

"He was making a new beginning."

"Because our names were in the book?"

"Because our names were the only ones in it."

"Plus Miranda."

She still showed nothing; the Boston cops *hadn't* been around. "Plus Miranda. But from what I understand there were no Bolivian addresses or numbers. He was here as somebody who had burned all his bridges . . ." She suddenly disliked her empty glass. "Oh."

"What's the matter?"

"There's your answer about his mother. If my theory is right, she must not have made it."

I felt like a heel. I'd come all the way to Boston chasing after a fancy built on mass murder, but she was still thinking of Paz in terms of people living and dying. I said something just for the sake of saying it. "By your theory, then, he came here for a green card."

She shrugged; she still didn't like thinking of a woman she'd never met as dead. "I suppose he came after what everyone else does—something new, something more."

"And you know this from a book you've only had described to you."

"I told you, Mr. Finley—I'm an expert on them."

And then Rosemary Stanton did something I hadn't expected: As a waitress walked by, she flagged her down for another daiquiri. I'd been so convinced she was going to leave any second I said no to another beer. I was still replying to questions that hadn't been asked.

Or vice versa.

Or something.

* * *

I stopped thinking of Rosemary Stanton as a delicate flower. The second daiquiri hadn't been out of politeness and hadn't been a habit; it had simply been what she had felt like. And she hadn't picked the Wooden Quarter for our meeting by chance, either: She owned the musical instruments store across the street.

"How does anyone end up owning a music store?"

"You have to be a terrible cellist, but you have to realize it's also too late to start a career in high finance or marine biology."

"Business doesn't seem to be booming," I said, glancing over at the somnolent shop.

"If I depended on walk-ins, there'd be no trade at all. Music schools and teachers recommend me. I make appointments by phone."

Had I been too hasty criticizing the Boston cops? Where better to keep an eye on her than from the pub? The thought made me feel better.

"Your line must involve you with all kinds," she said.

"You mean hotel room killers?"

"No, I didn't . . ."

"Just joking." And then I stopped joking for a few minutes, instead running down the roster of the clients being served by

Finley Investigations. I liked her for singling out the story of old Neil Riordan. "But there is one thing," she hedged. "Riordan himself might not feel as free and open to anything as you imagine him to be."

"I know. He could be dead in an alley somewhere."

"But you prefer to think otherwise."

"I'm not even sure I want to find him."

Her quiet surprise made me realize how much of an admission I'd made. She thought for a second, then sipped her drink confident about what she wanted to say. "Sure you do. You want to find him so you can see for yourself what he's been up to. What you're not sure you want to do is return him to his family."

She was right. "Like wanting to see the animals but not the zoo."

She frowned. "Is that the analogy?"

"It's what popped into my head. Sorry. I don't feel like watching my language with you."

I was still playing back that babbling when she gave me a gracious smile. Suddenly she seemed to know better than I did what I meant, what I might mean, or what I was pretending to mean. I was still trying to work out which was good and which was bad when she motioned again for the waitress and asked for the check. I muttered something about paying, refused her argument I was a guest in her city, and let her pay anyway.

On the way out, I took an extra look at the spidery redhead in the black leather jacket and the stocky black guy under a couple of layers of sweaters. They had been nursing beers from opposite ends of the bar since I'd walked in and hadn't spoken with anybody but the bartender. I bet on both as cops.

Twilight was sinking into nightfall as we walked over to the music shop. The sign said THE HIGH NOTE. Chiseled into the bottom of the glass door were the names N. FRUCHTER and R. STANTON.

"N. Fruchter?"

"That's the other way you end up owning a music store," she said, sticking her key in the lock. "Want to see?"

"Absolutely."

There was a flash from the parking garage at the end of the cul-de-sac. A slight man stood near the entrance applying a lighter to a cigarette. He didn't strike me as an employee. He was dressed in what looked like a tan summer suit under an old army coat. It was a bizarre combination, as though he had been vacationing in Boston since July, fallen asleep, then opened his eyes to discover that winter had come and he needed to get down to the Salvation Army for a heavy coat.

I thought Caribbean things. And then Latin American things. And then Bolivian things.

The shop was a mixture of mustiness and varnishes. It was small—two narrow aisles separated by a showcase of instrument attachments. A business desk sat against a rear wall, guitars and flutes dominated the items hooked to the side walls. In the far corner, to the right of the desk, there was a curtained off space. A light shone from under the curtain.

"Damn," Rosemary said. "I thought I turned that off."

My ferret jumped inside from the street before I could close the door behind us. "Stay here a second."

She didn't know what I was up to, and neither did I. Naturally, my Smith & Wesson was sitting in the middle drawer of my bureau in Bay Ridge. "What's the matter, Paul?"

"Just stay by the door a second."

As I moved toward the curtain, I told myself I had a dozen weapons within reach—clarinets, saxophones, trumpets. The only problem was, they were all behind glass. If I had stuck to the flute when I'd been a kid, my father suddenly nagged me, I would have had it with me and not needed anything else. Down to it, I had little choice but to sweep aside the curtain and let out a shout if I uncovered anything. The shout wasn't necessary. There was nothing behind the curtain but mussed up bedclothes on a cot, an old crate that had been converted into a bed table for a lamp and clock, and a toilet with a door ajar.

Oops, plus another door behind a scrim.

I cursed myself for being so out of practice and went over to the second door. It was one of those leaden exit doors with a bar that had always seemed so perfect for keeping fire victims trapped inside some movie house inferno. This one, though, offered no resistance at all because it was already resting on the tongue of its lock. Outside was a short alley that appeared to curve back around to the dead-end street.

"That was locked."

She had ignored my instructions to stay at the front, and I had a moment of panic that something besides my ferret was rushing in at that very moment. "You're sure?"

"It's always locked."

"See if anything's missing. I'll be right back."

She said something I didn't hear; I was just relieved to see she had at least closed the front door behind her.

So, I had to open it again, ducking my head in a half-flinch as though that would have done any good for any lurking ambush.

The slight man was still smoking in front of the garage. But as soon as I started heading toward him, he nonchalantly dropped his cigarette, stuck his hands into his army coat, and ambled into the garage. I would have ruined the whole effect by crying out to him.

But should have.

The garage interior wasn't the entrance with some timekeeper's booth that I had expected; there was nothing but a ramp snaking up to a second level. The place might have been designed by some hot car gang: an entrance on the far side of the building and the cul-de-sac for fast getaways. That was the brazenness of Boston crime for you.

Halfway up the ramp, I agreed the thumping I heard wasn't from my chest, but from a blaster somewhere at the back of the second level. The culprit was a garage man who was hosing down a red Sundance with the help of some hip-hop from the radio on the ground next to him. I couldn't see anyone else around, so I continued up the ramp to the third level. The further I got away from the radio, the more I wanted another sound to replace it—whatever the beat, whatever the lyrics. In the heavy silence of the third level that left only me to supply it.

"Come out, come out, wherever you are!"

So, it wasn't platinum rap. What bothered me more was that it was English, not Spanish.

"No good, bubba! We got a look at you! Come on down and pick up your FBI prize!"

"Help you, Mister?"

I wheeled around so fast that, even a good fifteen feet away, the tall black guy in the work clothes stepped back. Then he remembered the monkey wrench in his hand. "I asked you somethin'."

"Someone just come up here? Small, thin, in an army coat?"

He gave me a second to come up with a better story, didn't hear it, then just shook his head.

"You couldn't have missed him!"

"Well, I did. Or he took that."

I followed the guy's greasy index finger over to an elevator behind the first beam of the parking lanes. Even as I took it in, the IN-USE light was going off. "Where's that go?"

The garage man was beginning to enjoy me. "That was the green light so it went down to the main entrance. Got two doors, you know. Let's you go east and west dependin' on the floor. Clever, right? Have a nice day."

I wanted to say something smartass to him as he wandered away, but the only thing that occurred to me was a warning not to plagiarize my lyrics for any song he wrote in the future.

* * *

Rosemary Stanton sat behind her desk crossing her arms to her elbows, daring me to make her shudder. She wasn't convinced anyone, let alone a Latino with a tan summer suit under an army overcoat, had broken into the store because she couldn't remember the last time she had checked the back door; she was sure nothing had been stolen. She was aghast Hector Miranda and his relatives had been killed, and it was certainly curious the explosion had occurred so soon after Victor Paz had been killed. As for my close call in the university parking lot, she didn't know what to say.

"One thing I know, though. You're wrong about that woman in the leather jacket. She's there all the time. She's no cop."

"And the black guy in the sweaters?"

"I don't know *every*body in there."

"But it's good if he's a cop."

A small shiver finally came. "If I'm to believe all this."

"I have no reason to invent it, Rosemary."

"Then why not mention it earlier? You can't be that sure."

We were debating the wrong things. I moved away to the front of the store to light a cigarette and come back from another angle.

"What kind of a watchdog can the one in the sweaters be if people can walk in here to do what they please?"

I had no answer to that. I looked at the N. FRUCHTER written on the door again. "What about your partner? Has he mentioned any suspicious types hanging around lately?"

Her answer was nothing. When I turned back to her, she was giving both her arms a hard rub. "She, not he," she said finally, looking at the photo of herself with an older woman that was on the desk. "And she's been dead more than six months."

"I'm sorry."

"Norma wouldn't have noticed if the Bolivian army marched in here. Unless one of them had a tear in his bass drum."

She lifted her eyes to me so tiredly I felt a weight being passed to me across the store. She dared me to look at it, then look at it again. "You were more than friends?"

For a fraction of a second, she seemed to relax. But then she was back again behind her hard eyes. "If we hadn't been, that would be a helluva presumption on your part. But, yes, we were."

I had seen the movie before; it was called FINLEY OUT OF HIS DEPTH and it ended with Finley saying something oafish. So instead of wondering what Norma Fruchter had had that I didn't, I unleashed some smoke at the guitars on the walls. "I wish to hell someone would play!"

"That's what Norma always said. She said she felt surrounded by the potential of everything."

"And you?"

"Me? I was the practical genius because I remembered to pay the electric bill every month." She didn't want to talk about Norma Fruchter with me but didn't want to sound glib with the little she said, either. "I loved her very much. We were together seven years."

I nodded, and she seemed satisfied with that. Then she thought of something for distracting both of us. "Let me ask your advice," she said, getting up and meandering out from behind the desk. "She's gone more than six months now, almost seven. When does it get morbid for me to leave her name on the door like that?"

"Maybe the second time you ask yourself that question."

"You sound like you're speaking from experience."

I remembered the morning at the Professor's old house vividly. It had been Jennifer's birthday, and I had opened my eyes with a clear decision. "Insurance policies, credit cards, joint bank accounts—I had them all changed by noon."

"One fell swoop?"

"One fell swoop. Not to do it seemed obscene. Like I was saying my wife might have been dead for me, but she'd never be dead for MasterCard or Chase Manhattan."

She was still undecided as she looked out at the Wooden Quarter. A second later she looked back at me as if the time had come to end the game we were playing. "The police aren't really sure of any of this, are they?"

"No."

"This Miranda bombing . . . I mean, I'm not doubting you. But I talked to Victor Paz for a half-hour! Goddamit, Paul, I'm an American citizen blessed by God!"

She wanted me to laugh with her, but I didn't get the chance. One second she was trying to giggle, the next her bottom lip was trembling. And then I was holding the shudders that came from every part of her body. Hitmen didn't have mothers who died in hospitals, I wanted to tell her.

* * *

The hours passed. She told me about her need to get away from the months she had spent nursing Norma Fruchter, about a never-ending tour through Peru, Bolivia, Chile, and Argentina with five middle-aged couples and an old priest who had—jokingly, suspiciously, or conversationally—wanted to know why she hadn't married. I told her about Jennifer and Susan, then about a 15-year-old kid named Tommy Reynolds who had been hit on by some of Long Island's randiest swells for their weekend sex games, had developed second thoughts about his pastime, and had then been killed by a high school buddy so he wouldn't blow the fun for everybody. She told me about returning from her South American trip to find Norma Fruchter still dead and the air in the High Note still clotted with the years when she had been alive and healthy. I told her about Ellen Miles and my other Major Cases friends who didn't like me accusing them of caving into political pressures on the job.

She didn't want to go out for dinner. She didn't want to because she didn't see me as a social acquaintance for restaurant meals and because she thought the man in the army coat had violated her store and she wanted to stay on the premises to hold its hand. So, we ordered Chinese and camped out on the floor, listening some more to the silence of the instruments on the walls and to whatever there was that still refused to be said about ourselves. I didn't think I was kidding myself. Rosemary Stanton was a haven I hadn't thought about needing again after the Great Breakthrough of leaving the Professor's house and moving to Brooklyn. She was a halfway house I'd skipped in haste. I didn't have to prove anything to her because she wasn't making even her loneliness available for more than matching notes, and that seemed to raise the price of my own to where I couldn't cover it casually. Dumplings and beef broccoli seemed like the perfect last supper for all those squeamish emotions.

"What happened to the boy who killed this Tommy Reynolds?"

"Reduced manslaughter charge."

"And the publicity?"

"Some names got mentioned, but not fatally enough. Sometimes I think all I accomplished was to make sure the kid sent to jail wouldn't have a pot to piss in when he gets out. If I'd kept quiet, maybe all the good Long Island folk—the Hamptonites and the Operation Rescuers and the political machines—maybe they would've been able to hold the killing over the head of the poor son of a bitch, go on manipulating him."

"Well, isn't that something?"

"That I saved him from that fate and helped get him convicted, instead? You better ask him. Maybe he'd prefer to be manipulated and blackmailed and threatened if it got him more of an existence than as some gas station jockey. I have no idea, Rosemary. You do what you think is right, but ticker tape parades aren't part of the deal."

She smiled and leaned over to brush something off my sweater. "You already have enough lint there."

It was after midnight when I couldn't ignore her yawns anymore and announced I was heading back to New York. She was grateful I said it first and put off any further delays by saying she was going to stay in the store rather than go home. I thought she was right not to worry about the guy from the garage, at least for one night. Army Coat knew he had been spotted, and there was still the cop in the sweaters across the street in the pub. Why *not* sleep in the back?

I walked out into the cold with the garbage from our meal. The Wooden Quarter was still awake, but barely. The rear entrance to the garage down the street had been sealed. I threw the trash into the sidewalk can and turned around to find her staring again at Norma Fruchter's name on the door. "Thanks for the tip," she said. "Today was actually the hundredth time I'd asked myself."

"The mailman will always know where to drop off the bills."

"A good argument for leaving it there. I can be Rosemary Stanton for the good mail and Norma can get all the bills."

It had been meant as nothing more than Good Night talk, but it jostled something in my head.

"What's the matter?"

"What you just said."

"About Norma?"

"I think so . . . Well, whatever. Breezes in the steeple."

"Now you've lost me."

"One of the Professor's sayings. The breezes that blow through the steeple, but not hard enough to ring the bell."

She looked relieved I hadn't meant something specific about her and Norma. How much longer would she be listening for that kind of thing?

"Sure you'll be all right here?"

"I use the cot a lot. Sometimes it seems more . . . controllable than my own bed."

"Okay, then. We'll talk."

"Of course."

I kissed her hurriedly on the cheek and got away before I had to inscribe any last image of her on my mind. I counted ten, fifteen, twenty yards—all the way up to my car—before she closed and locked the door behind me. For good measure, I added a few more paces before I then went around the car and across to the bar.

There were only a few singles left in the Wooden Quarter—all of them looking as resigned to their surroundings as Rachel and Johnny Yeager back at the Green Fox. Granted my discovery—the black guy with all the sweaters—wasn't likely to pull a double shift on his barstool, but where the hell was his relief man? Not counting the bartender, no one in the place looked capable of dealing with anything heavier than a beer mug.

"Last call, fella."

I waved off the bartender and went back outside. It had to be the bartender, I told myself: What better stakeout cover from a saloon? Then I saw the summons on my windshield and lost my last illusion. I made out the words Unauthorized, Parking, and Zone. Any jury would have to conclude I wasn't too good at reading signs.

I pocketed the summons and got into the car. As I began to warm up, I told myself Rosemary didn't need a cop watching her anyway. Cops—even Boston cops—knew their business. If they had decided Bernstein's call had been an overreaction, they had probably had their reasons.

None of which occurred to me.

I lighted a cigarette and moved the car from the cul-de-sac to the cross street. I parked where I had a clear home plate view of the music store and the garage. I gave myself until I finished my cigarette, then until the Wooden Quarter closed. I think I would have taken off as soon as the bartender and the last two skels came out if not for the damn squeaking of the cello. One of the skels made a crack I couldn't hear, all three of them had a laugh behind looks over at the High Note, then they all wandered off in their parkas like a trio of lumberjacks that had just left another slain tree laying in the forest. I hated them.

On the other hand, Rosemary Stanton had been right about giving up her cellist's career. My taste in classical music runs to those Brits who scored all that epic music for Hollywood in the 1950s and 1960s, but I didn't need Beethoven sitting next to me to know I was listening to a Sunday musician. There were stretches of music—pure music—when I pictured dandies in satin clothes and powdered wigs sitting in a European drawing room; then some scratch got me back to looking at the dashboard or counting the cigarettes left in the pack. It was music for company, for consolation, maybe for just feeling modestly talented before going to bed.

She took more than an hour to go to bed.

I knew I hadn't proven anything by waiting until the neighborhood had collapsed under its own fatigue. What was to prevent Army Coat from making another pass at her as soon as I started back to New York? My commitment to her had lasted barely longer than my cigarettes had.

I couldn't help that.

And there was one other thing. Listening to her melancholy descend over the darkened pub and the sealed garage, I remembered what she had said about getting Norma Fruchter's bills at the store simply because Norma's name was still on the door. I had yet to figure out why, but heading toward the turnpike I thought of Phil Ortega and had a general idea of how my name had ended up in Victor Paz's address book.

FOUR

I didn't get around to my answering machine until I rolled out of bed at the noon the next day. The first and fifth calls were the Professor finding awkward ways of asking whether I was dead. The second was from Mrs. Morgan's lawyer, reminding me he could use anything at all before the next hearing on Tuesday. There were a couple of other messages threatening work if my fees were reasonable. I was so sure the highlight of the tape would be Bernstein wondering why I hadn't been around that I was caught doubly off guard by a happy Mrs. Riordan reporting that her husband had returned home after "looking up some old Navy pals." Rosemary Stanton had been wrong: I *had* wanted to bring Neil Riordan home because then I could have also seen the joy Mrs. Riordan had shared only with my answering machine. As it was, I had spent a lot of time searching for somebody I was never going to see.

There was nothing at all from Bernstein so I did the calling. My indignation over the invisible watch on Rosemary would have been more effective if he hadn't sounded as irritated as I was. "I called Vincent about it as soon as I got off the phone with you," he insisted.

"I thought you were calling the Boston cops."

Only a fraction of his sigh seemed directed at me. "Get with the program, Finley. If this isn't Federal, what is?"

"Meaning you're out of the loop?"

That got his full attention. "Give me a description of this guy hanging around the store."

I would have been more helpful if I'd taken more notice of Army Coat's features and less of his clothes.

"How high up did you say you got in Mineola?"

"I was half a block away!"

Bernstein backed off; he was still simmering about Vincent. "Okay. Running anywhere today I should know about? Los Angeles, maybe?"

His sarcasm made me decide. On the drive down from Boston, I'd made up my mind to confront Ortega as soon as I got to the campus for my next class. But why wait another day and a half? I had too many questions, and if the near-miss in the parking lot and Army Coat meant anything, I didn't have infinity for getting the answers.

Snow flurries, the radio weatherman kept saying, and by Garden City, the snow was flurrying enough to weigh down my wipers. My loafers never felt more amphibious as I made my way over the parking lot to Ortega's office. Naturally, he wasn't there, so I had to mush on to the building where, per his secretary, he was giving a class. I got madder with every step and might have worked myself up to titanic self-righteousness if, a few feet from my destination, I hadn't almost taken a header. A passing coed made it worse by asking if I was okay, her tone suggesting I should never venture out in the snow without my walker.

Ortega was holding forth in an amphitheater only slightly smaller than Madison Square Garden. Slipping inside through the rear door at the second level, I counted a good 60 or 70 disciples spread around below me. The ones not taking notes seemed afraid of losing eye contact with him. It wasn't exactly like my class, where most paid attention but where two bozos sitting in the back had yet to get over the neat designs their watchbands left on their wrists.

I got in just in time for some last words on someone named John Palmstruck, whom Ortega described as a Swedish con man who had been the first to popularize paper money in Europe—and the first swindler to be jailed for paper currency fraud. Staring at the name PALMSTRUCK on the board, I wondered if it too had come from Victor Paz's book.

Ortega spotted me as soon as I walked in, then kept his eyes elsewhere until the bell rang and everybody headed for the lower-level door. With the last kid gone he grabbed an eraser and went to work on his giant PALMSTRUCK. "Need another book?"

"What I need is to know who Victor Paz was."

If I hadn't stopped halfway down the amphitheater steps, I would have missed his shoulder slump between swipes at the blackboard. "I was counting on you to forget that by now."

I told Norma Fruchter to rest in peace: She had accomplished a last good work on earth. "Yeah, well."

Ortega noticed that the lower-level door had been left ajar and hurried over to close it. Only then was he ready to look at me. "Know the stupidest part, Paul? Victor Paz was nobody! I hardly remembered him when you started talking about him. I mean it. He was just a guy."

"Just a guy who thought you were Paul Finley."

He had an endless supply of embarrassed shrugs as he strolled back to the desk. "I met him in Bogota over Christmas. I guess that's what I made him think, yeah. You never did anything like that?"

"Tell people I'm someone else? You mean it's a common thing?"

"It can happen."

"To you."

"Jesus, you make it sound like the crime of the century! Look, I run into this guy at a hotel bar down there. We talk, who remembers about what. I don't like him; I don't dislike him. He's just this guy in a bar talking about how he can't find work in his own country, hasn't had much better luck in Colombia, and wants to go to America someday. I buy him a couple of drinks, wish him all the luck in the world. Somewhere along the line, I suppose I tell him to look me up if he ever makes it."

"He did."

I was the dense student who had to have it explained more simply. "Okay, but it isn't like I wanted him showing up on my doorstep someday. What for? So, he could remind me of the ass I'd made of myself in a Bogota bar one night?"

"How did you did make an ass of yourself, Phil?"

Suddenly he was more interested in the snow coming down harder outside the window. "Nothing. The way I do at Joe's sometimes. My marathon mouth after too much booze."

"But why me? If you didn't want him ever showing up at your place, you could've been Bill Smith from Toledo."

"Yeah, I know."

"So?"

"Jesus, this sounds so jerky when you try to explain it! How could I tell him I was Bill Smith? If he did manage to get up here, I'd be *somewhat* responsible, wouldn't I? At least if he called you, I figured I'd hear about it and have the option of seeing him again, give him a hand if necessary."

I must have looked as stupefied as I felt. Even after having felt so clever about relating the address book to Rosemary's comment about getting bills in somebody else's name, I couldn't fix Ortega in anything I was familiar with. The closest I came were the aliases panicky johns gave Vice after being nabbed with hookers.

He came back from the window to the bottom of my aisle. He wanted to give me one of his bashful salmon smiles but knew better than to try it. "Look, this stuff about the cops and everything, you trying to figure it all out—granted I should have told you right away. But I couldn't admit it that night at the Professor's, not in front of all those people."

"I have a phone. I'm on campus twice a week. If you remember, I was even in your office the other day."

"I know, I know. But you looked . . . well, like you even enjoyed it as a mystery."

"What're you saying? I should thank you?"

Arms in the air like Barrymore. "No! What you should do is be happy you're not a creep like me! That what you want to hear?"

Yes, I thought, but also much more than that. For instance, I wanted to hear something that might make sense to the severed pieces of Hector Miranda's family. "And the rest?"

"What rest?"

"The part that has nothing to do with you being embarrassed in front of Barbara and Angela. You said you made an ass of yourself with Paz. How? It wouldn't have been that speech about your little Indio, would it? That what you and Paz talked about?"

Bullseye. He went from abject to alert so fast I wanted to kick myself for accepting even a slither of his apology. I saw it completely. Ortega and Paz sitting at a blond wood bar. Moving their knees a lot because the bar hadn't been built with knees in mind. Barely taking in the piano player who was winding down with a medley from *Cats* or the exotic fish in the aquarium behind the bar. And in the middle of it all? "You got boozy with him. You assured him you were brothers under the skin no matter who'd paid for your airline tickets and hotel room. What were you afraid of, Phil? He'd show up here and ask you to help him stow the grenades?"

"I told you he was a nobody."

"But who perked up when you told him about your Indio."

"A nobody, Finley. A guy in a bar."

"A hotel bar? He couldn't have been that broke. You're not that sociable with your average panhandler, are you?"

"You don't have to be destitute to be oppressed."

"Good to know it. Why don't you tell that to those people blown all around Jackson Heights? Victor Paz wasn't destitute and he wasn't down on his luck, Phil. What he was was your bullshit."

It was as much as my mad was good for; a word more and I would have started sputtering. I spotted a piece of paper on the desk, went down to it, and scribbled Bernstein's phone number.

"You're disappointed, aren't you?" he said. "You liked having this little mystery in your life."

I recognized the tone. The police shrink I'd seen after Jennifer's accident had always been telling me I was defensive when I disagreed with her. "Save the brain massage for yourself. This is Lieutenant Allen Bernstein's number. Call him today and explain all this."

His hands stayed in his jacket pockets. "How can I help him any more than you did?"

"First off, you're helping *me*—by getting an FBI slug off my back. Bernstein, he's going to have his faith restored in Nassau cops. And maybe you can even see your way to painting him a picture of the when and where of your drinks with Paz. Take the fucking number."

"I won't be pushed, Paul."

I thought about shoving the phone number through his teeth, but I really didn't want to touch him so I just left it on the desk. "Don't call him by tonight and I will. You got zero to gain."

I almost made it to the door before his smarting spat back. "Zero—what you're an expert in. A lot of people out here don't like you, Finley."

"You've made that point before."

"But they can't touch you here. You have new respectability on this campus. Their own kids are being taught by you. They hate it, but they can't do anything about it. You're shoving it back in their faces. Understand what I'm telling you?"

I did. All the wanting I'd seen in Phil Ortega had been for a corduroy jacket with elbow patches, after all.

"You're blowing it with me, Finley."

"Too bad. I really did want to be *somewhat* responsible."

It wasn't until I hit the front steps of the building and felt my wet loafers protesting that they weren't up for another dive into the snow that I slowed down my brain. My exit line had been too hollow. Ortega calling Bernstein to set one detail right was neither here nor there. I still had something to lose, and it had nothing to do with Long Island society.

So why couldn't I put my finger on what it was, exactly?

* * *

I spent the next day earning my money on the Morgan custody case by finally tracking down Patrick Hardy. He was a Woodside pharmacist who shared information with a private investigator as enthusiastically as he sold rubbers to the Catholic teenagers in the neighborhood. But he made up for his general leeriness with an outburst that he didn't even know who the hell Mrs. Morgan was, but had volunteered his deposition about her alcoholic habits because one of the other notarized liars ("a gentleman I've always been proud to call a friend") had asked him to "help one of our own." The lawyer was ecstatic over my find. He couldn't wait to call Mrs. Morgan with a promise of setting off major fireworks at the Tuesday hearing. I was a little more skeptical. The purity in me leaves me uneasy about winning points just because the other team is taking its Gatorade from Paleolithic wells. The lawyer told me I should enjoy life more. And by the way, had I made any progress in getting that money from the deadbeat Martin Lucchese?

Twenty-four hours after my scene with Ortega I still hadn't heard from Bernstein, so I called his office. He was out, but McGill anticipated my question by confirming that Ortega had called. If it was explicit vindication I was looking for, what I got was the tone of a detective sergeant dismissing a witness as being less helpful than had been hoped.

After class that night I dropped in on the Professor. Ortega wasn't there, and I would have had a new definition of gall if he had been, but Angela Balestrini was sitting on the couch debating Sid Feldman about the European Community. When she raised her eyes to me, managing a smile through something about the status of the old Soviet satellites, I decided to pay more attention to Bulgaria's economic problems. Even with a blouse on, she still seemed to be wearing her spaghetti straps.

For a half-hour or so I was aloft on the idea that I'd turned a few corners. I had cleared myself with Bernstein (and presumably with Vincent), spat my bile with Ortega, and, ideal conclusions or not, closed the file on Neil Riordan and come close to doing the same with the Morgans. What better reward than the realization that Angela Balestrini didn't have to come as a package with the Ortegas? She acted as though I had lost some of the same tethers. Maybe I had, maybe I hadn't, but I was determined to drive her home that night. I even stopped drinking after the first scotch.

The Professor had never started. He looked agitated, barely rising to the bait of deliberately outlandish contentions directed at him. I didn't find out what was bothering him until he caught me coming out of the bathroom. "Got a minute?" He went straight down the hall to his bedroom and closed the door after us. "You can take that with you," he growled, pointing to Ortega's book on his dresser.

"I don't need it. I told you, I talked to him."

He eased himself down on the bed as if his back was against the idea. "Yeah, you told me."

"What's the matter? You look like you're passing iron."

"When you're my age you can tell me what I'm passing. What I want to know is what you're going to do now."

"About what?"

"About this Paz business, what else?"

"Nothing. Bernstein knows the story."

"Swell. And the people who still think you're Ortega?"

The thought had occurred to me, of course. But aside from deterring me from going down to my laundry room after midnight, the thought didn't seem worth much. "What's bugging you, Joe?"

He stared over at BOLIVIA ABOVE GROUND without actually seeing it. "I figured you for the cop in the family. I read the papers, watch the tube—not a goddamn word about what happened to that cabbie. Paz? He's last month's news. What's bugging me, Paul, is that you're sitting outside ogling that nifty lady with the BA accent like you don't have a care in the world. Me, I think you got plenty and this Bernstein isn't helping you keep your guard up."

"The guy's as hamstrung . . ."

"Yeah, yeah, I know. The Feds and the cops and all that crap. A regular Guelph and Ghibelline fratricide between professionals. Except when they're covering each other's tailbones. Get over that mythology, Finley. You're out of the cops long enough."

I didn't know what to say. It seemed like a continuation of the anger he had shown the night I had given him Ortega's book and still seemed to be related to more than the mystery of Victor Paz. "How about A-B-C, Joe? So, we'll both know what you're talking about."

"I don't like this news blackout. Ask me, they've tied you and your friend in Boston to the stake like goats. You need some protection."

Had I made him too much a part of Finley Investigations when I had been operating from the basement of the old house? "And you got this where—from Ortega's book?"

"No. What I got from that was remembering what kind of people the Ortegas are. And that reminded me of what kind your Vincents are."

"You're losing me, Joe."

He pursed his lips over a final hesitation, then reached into his shirt pocket and came out with a slip of paper. "I want you to call this guy tomorrow. He's expecting to hear from you."

The paper contained the name NEARING and a Manhattan number. "Who the hell is Nearing?"

"He's not FBI and he gets around more than this Bernstein. Talk to him. You want to know more from me afterward, you can ask. But frankly, I'd prefer you didn't."

"Joe . . .!"

The red started to show around his ears. "I'm telling you to be curious in a profitable way. The rest is horseshit. Can you respect that?"

"Sure. Then I'll walk out of here thinking Joe Carroll's some kind of spook. Maybe always has been."

For the first time all night, he smiled easily. "That might flatter me in some perverse way." The smile vanished again. "But I'm no spook. I'm just somebody who's attended enough funerals and doesn't want to go to another one unless they're talking about me. Can you do me that favor?"

He knew he had me. "And when I meet this Nearing, should I tell him it's nice to CIA him?"

He made another project of getting back on his feet. "I think you need some basic information you're not getting from other people. Who knows? It might even put some common sense in your skull."

I watched him go over to the door under siege from CIA fantasies and a couple of others that refused to take shape.

"And throw that goddamn book out!"

I stood staring at NEARING and the Manhattan number until someone in the living room let out a whoop. The next voice I heard was the Professor's. He was tearing into Sid Feldman about Trotsky and Stalin.

***

I drove Angela to the Ortega place in Sea Cliff. My timing was one day off: She was moving to an apartment in Hempstead the next day.

"I intended moving anyway, but after last night . . ."

"What happened last night?"

I had to keep my eye on an oncoming van, but I could feel her scrutiny. "I did not hear it all, but I should not have heard any of it. It reminded me I was a guest too long. Phil was upset. He kept saying he had been 'humiliated.' That was the word he kept using. And your name was mentioned." The van passed, but I wouldn't have minded having to watch out for another one. "Was what happened necessary?"

"I thought so."

She refolded her hands on her lap and said nothing for a long moment. Then: "Barbara said he should fire you."

"He won't have to."

"You don't like what you are doing?"

"Actually, it's been fun. I've learned as much as the kids have."

"That is unfortunate." She was waiting for me with an evil smile. "If the student must do all the work in addition to paying all that tuition, he should learn more than he teaches."

"Funny."

"You disagree?"

"I never claimed I was a teacher. You are."

She took to pondering that distinction in silence for the rest of the ride. I let her off a couple of doors down from Ortega's colonial house because it seemed like a good compromise between having her jump out while I sped past and walking her right up to the front door. "Maybe we can get a drink when you're settled in Hempstead."

She nodded but was still back on another thought. "Academics here are different than in my country. They are much more portable."

"Portable?"

She was more interested in her point than in faulty transliterations. "Here they seem to carry everything with them—their ambitions, their self-esteem, even their humiliations. In my country, a *profesor* has an invisible place where he leaves all such things while he is being authoritative in his university position."

"And what have you left in this invisible place?"

She still wasn't impressed by my lame gambits. "I was talking about Phil. It is like he carries his title and position in his pocket like scraps of paper. And sometimes he misplaces the right scrap. Do you understand?"

"I don't think so."

She smiled. "I think you do. You are like Phil that way—you don't trust the invisible places, either. You fear you may not find them when you go back to retrieve what you left in them."

For some reason, I thought of a music store in a cul-de-sac.

She wrote down the address of her Hempstead apartment, then got out and half-ran, half-skidded to the Ortegas' front door. Something told me I'd looked even more disjointed with every step I had taken lately.

* * *

Nearing's first name was Roger, and that might have been a couple of facts or a couple of lies. He was in his late fifties or early sixties and had exactly one layer of wavy gray hair. He might have been a securities executive—the kind who never rises all the way to the top, but who always has the right information handy to remind his superiors of something they have overlooked. Roger Nearing the securities executive, I told myself, had a house in Connecticut, two kids out of college, blood pressure that wouldn't drop as much as it should, and a wife who picked her spots to sneak low-calorie food on his plate.

Then there was Roger Nearing the Professor's friend who liked getting together at an Upper Broadway McDonald's because it evoked the shabbiness of adventures he wasn't involved in anymore. He let me get the coffees and bring them over to a window table.

"So how is Joe?"

"Retired."

"The body, maybe. Never the mind."

"You know him from the university?"

He picked up his plastic cup with practically all ten fingers and slurped. I took the hint. "He thinks you can tell me a few things."

I was forgiven. "The Bolivians? Fill me in."

I hadn't come that far to be evasive, so I did. As soon as I finished, Nearing reached over the table to pull back my jacket. "This is a chat between strangers, right?"

"If I was wired, you'd be in trouble already."

"Not really. But amenities are amenities." He sat back. "Paz?"

"He seems to be the starting point."

"A hitman. Like they told you."

Why did one point for Frank Vincent feel like one less for me?

"Miranda? Unless the pods took over his body he was the Dominican who came here with his parents and sister in 1981, tried to make a go of a bodega with his family, saw the store go under, then got a hack license. In short, a cab driver who picked up his politics from *El Diario*."

That felt like minus two points; I put up a fight just for the hell of it. "Maybe Miranda wasn't the important man. Maybe it was one of his cousins in the house and he was just a reference point for contacting the cousin."

If nothing else, Nearing looked at me as though I weren't a *total* idiot. "No. But it was a thought for a few minutes."

"Okay. What about this assassination business?"

Nearing wasn't sure he liked my fast food counter attitude, but he hadn't come so far to be evasive, either. He reached into his jacket pocket for an envelope. Naturally, it had no markings. He removed several photos, keeping them close to his chest so I wouldn't forget who was dealing. "Number one, Ambassador Juan Montaldo Reyes."

As curious as I was about the picture on the table, I suddenly had second thoughts about sitting in the window. "Relax," he said, thinking I was funny again. "I'm just turning another pusher against his supplier."

And enjoying the image a little too much. But I turned my attention back to the photograph. Ambassador Montaldo was a broad-faced man with a black mustache, frameless glasses, and too much forehead.

"Former Air Force commander. Booted out during the Banzer regime—the second one. There have been lots of Banzer regimes.

Montaldo's the ballroom dancer who knocks on the president's door with a look of shock a few minutes before the tanks set out to surround the presidential palace. He's turned that sense of timing into a self-importance second to nobody's. But it's worked. His image as a nonaligned problem solver has given him credibility in places like the OAS and UN. You eliminate Montaldo, you eliminate Bolivia's chief statesman abroad."

"So they can't have the Keystone Kops guarding him."

Nearing spat his second picture. The crooked nose and double chin showed a boxer gone to seed, but the beady eyes said his unpleasantness was still in flower. "Antonio Becquer. Head of mission security. If you're defending the goal line against Victor Paz, Becquer's your goalie. One of the FBI's proudest exchange program graduates."

"Good for us."

"Becquer's a cop version of Montaldo. No matter how many custard pies get thrown around, they never quite smear his clothes."

"But he and Montaldo hit it off?"

"For now," he said, repressing a smile.

I started thinking I was learning too much and not nearly enough. But that thought immediately tasted more watery than my coffee when he dealt out the third picture. It was Army Coat from Boston.

"Manuel Lerico. Becquer's right hand. Unadorned thug."

"I know him."

"How?"

When I told him, he looked interested but not fascinated. "Maybe Vincent's right on that, too," he said.

"Fine. But maybe somebody should do something about it."

"Tell Vincent."

"I'm telling you."

I heard the answer before I heard the words. "I'm here as a favor to Joe Carroll, not in any investigative capacity. And this one?"

It was the last card in his deck and gave me a pair. Victor Paz looked as anonymous in what was probably a passport photo as he had looked on the morgue gurney. "Paz."

Nearing hesitated a second, then scooped up all the pictures and put them back in his envelope. "Okay, then. What you got seems to be what they told you. Paz came here to do Montaldo. Becquer and Lerico were waiting for him. They took him out, then Miranda. Lerico in Boston suggests an intention to go after you and Stanton, too. That parking lot thing probably wasn't an accident."

"So we're bait and should be happy about it?"

He thought that was funny. "Notice any fishermen?"

"What's that mean?"

He shrugged. "You say nobody was watching Stanton. They give your place a bomb squad quickie, then leave the rest to local command cars. If you're bait, who's watching when the line gets yanked?"

The question trickled through my stomach like displaced mucous.

"Anybody else?"

I'd almost forgotten. "Philip Ortega."

Nearing shook his head. "Joe mentioned him. Just an academic hustler. He may deliver laundry lists back and forth, but he gets his hottest stuff from around the water cooler like a lot of other people who think they're insiders. Your problems aren't with the publish-or-perish crowd, they're with . . . well, you make the joke."

"You don't exactly reassure people, Nearing."

He didn't think of it as a fatal flaw; he was more interested in locating a basket for his plastic cup. "You pass on the information about Lerico?"

"I didn't have a name."

"Now you do. In your place, I'd pass it along. Fastest. Ask me where to pass it on, that's your call."

He would have left me sitting there and gone straight from the garbage can near the door to the street if I hadn't followed after him. Twilight was dropping over Broadway, and a clamminess had settled in under the cold. I was agitated enough to irritate him by asking what subway he was taking, but instead remembered something more important. "Joe seems to think you owe him. Why?"

"He say that?"

"Not in so many words."

He weighed his answer as he buttoned his lined raincoat to the top. "Once upon a time the Professor was in a bad place and he had to do something he didn't want to do," he said finally. "He ended up doing even more than what was asked of him. Nice seeing you, Finley."

He didn't offer his hand, just pivoted and headed toward the #1 stop at 86th Street. I thought again about annoying him on general principles. But then he stepped off the sidewalk and grabbed a cab going downtown. At least I'd saved myself one inane gesture.

* * *

What had I learned? Standing in the middle of Broadway, not too much occurred to me except where Bernstein was concerned. Maybe it was a kneejerk reaction from my cop days, as the Professor had said, but I had to trust somebody and better the fat man than Vincent. Even without my own problems with Vincent, there had been Nearing's reference to how Becquer had been trained by the FBI. The longer I stood in the middle of the sidewalk drawing looks from those who had to go around me, the louder I heard Nearing's message of STAY AWAY FROM VINCENT.

I walked down to the 79th Street stop to give myself a few more minutes to think of an alternative to calling on Bernstein. I couldn't think of any. I might not have needed two pros like Becquer and Lerico the way Montaldo did, but I needed help from somewhere. I arrived on the 79th Street platform just as the downtown local was pulling in. I took that as an omen of heading in the right direction.

I reached the station house just as half the command was scrambling out on an emergency call. Bernstein and McGill were hurrying down the stairs from the second floor. I thought she was being tactful about not getting too far ahead of him, but she didn't have much diplomacy left over for her expression when she saw me in front of the receiving desk. "Not now, Finley," Bernstein seconded, his breath coming in fits. "We got a hostage situation on our hands."

That ripped it. "Great. So did I."

The fat man calculated quickly: A minute of being detained would also let him recover his wind. He nodded for McGill to go ahead. She gave me another demerit but continued out the door. "What's the problem?"

"The guy I saw outside Stanton's store, his name is Manuel Lerico. That ring any bells?"

For a second I thought he was going to be a sore loser. But then he was more concerned about walking me out of the way of two blues scampering outside to their car. "Been working overtime?"

"Happens when I get a feeling no one else's watching my back."

"Sure it was Lerico?"

"Absolutely."

He nodded. "Okay. I want you to do me a favor. I want you to go home right now. I'll be by to see you later."

He looked so genuinely crestfallen about something I could say nothing as he brought up the rear of the stampede out the door. I didn't even remind him that home was Bay Ridge, right across the border from Iowa. I knew he knew that. And was still going to drop by.

* * *

The ride home on the **R** was its usual delight. The highlight was a bag lady sprawled across the seats next to me suddenly coming awake, spitting in my general direction for trying to steal her shopping bag of rags, then immediately falling back to sleep. A lug in a stocking cap across from me shook his head in wonder at the joys of the big city. I thought he was more of a pain in the ass than the old woman.

I sneaked a look at the Green Fox without going in. Most of the usuals were in place and Cynthia was eating at the back. Rachel peered over at the window in what I hoped was a half-second after I had ducked. A cat or two had seen some hallway action in my building since I'd left in the afternoon, and I couldn't get into the elevator fast enough. Maybe if I had been thinking of something besides neutering the tom population of Bay Ridge, I wouldn't have reacted so lethargically to the body that was suddenly behind me and pushing me to the car's far wall.

"Mr. Finley."

Aside from a concentrated spearmint gum odor, Manuel Lerico up close didn't offer much more than Manuel Lerico at the end of a cul-de-sac or Manuel Lerico in a photograph. He was bone thin under his army overcoat, with the glimmering eyes of somebody who looked starved on more than a physical level. As he pushed a button with the hand he took out of his coat pocket, I told myself I had been murdered by cat spray. "You know me, I believe."

"Lerico."

He hit the Stop button. The abrupt halt wasn't abrupt enough, even if I had been ready to make a move against the second hand that remained in his pocket. "You must leave New York, Mr. Finley."

I hadn't realized how much I'd considered myself already dead until he jutted his chin at me demanding a response. "I just did."

"Not just for a few hours. And not Boston."

"Why?"

"It is beyond your comprehension," he said, sounding as if he had memorized the phrase at Berlitz. "Just go."

A nerve or two began functioning again. "I suppose that was the message you wanted to give Rosemary Stanton, too."

"Yes. But you prevented me."

I felt more murk coming but had little choice except to step into it. "Why worry about us? You didn't worry about Paz or the Miranda family."

"It is beyond your comprehension."

"That's for sure."

"Will you go?"

"What do you expect me to say—no?"

"I'm interested in what you do, not what you say."

There was something wrong with our conversation: We should not have been having it. But I was hardly going to point it out to him with his hand still in his pocket. "How long am I supposed to leave for?"

"Two, maybe three weeks," he said promptly.

"For what? . . . Right. It's beyond my comprehension."

I hadn't seen the glare he gave me since my last Dracula movie. "Take this as a grave warning, Mr. Finley. You have no reason to ignore it."

"You trying to tell me you had nothing to do with killing Paz or that bombing in Queens?"

"I am telling you only to leave. Tomorrow, please."

He hit the lobby button so quickly he could have done a dozen other things with the same hand and I would have been too slow to anticipate them. I knew Nearing hadn't exaggerated his specialty.

"Believe me, Mr. Finley, I don't want anything to happen, either."

He had a dancer's spryness in getting from the elevator to the front door. I'd never had a chance of catching him in that Boston garage.

* * *

A couple of scotches later I'd come to several conclusions about Paul Finley. First, he had lost more than one step since saying goodbye to Major Cases. Second, Victor Paz wasn't a Bolivian seaman, he was the Lost Forest from that Disney cartoon where none of the trees was what it seemed and where doddering detectives couldn't work out east, west, north, or south. Third, everybody I'd met lately liked how I didn't know which way was up. I wasn't bait, I was the muddy riverbank all the fishermen were slogging through without a second thought.

And the Professor was slogging through me like everyone else. I'd put off calling him precisely because I didn't feel like telling him Nearing had been informative, hearing some grunt of satisfaction and then a click in my ear. Whatever the hell he had done with Nearing, he not only had never mentioned it to me, he had never told Jennifer (or I would have heard *something*). So much secrecy plus Nearing's knowledge of Bolivian embassy personnel added up to the CIA or some other spook club like it. But how the hell did Joe Carroll get involved with that crowd? And what did that have to do with the old man's throbbing contempt for Ortega?

I got tired of the ugly questions. I didn't feel like examining all the profitable activities of Finley Investigations, either. So, I ended up doing what I rarely do—camping down in front of the TV set and watching those asinine sitcoms where the actors compete at yelling at one another, you can hear the punchline rolling down from the top of Everest, and laugh tracks of long-dead tourists explode like Krakatoa at the hilarity of it all. It wasn't comforting knowing I wasn't the only pathetic shit in the country.

The 11 o'clock news was coming on when my door buzzer sounded. For once I managed a clear thought and got my Smith & Wesson from the dresser before answering. Few as my guests had been since moving in, none had gotten through the vestibule and up to my floor without first calling up.

"It's Bernstein!"

It was that kind of day: If Joe Louis or Ali had been fighting, I would have bet every cent on the Bum of the Month. And Bernstein just loved seeing my .38 over the door chain. "Nice, very nice."

I didn't want to let him in. The scotches and sitcoms had gutted my interest in Victor Paz for the evening. Besides, I had the illusion that talking with Lerico had put everything on hold for a few hours.

"Feel like taking a drive?"

"At this hour? No."

Sometimes even fat men can look drawn—especially with a single table lamp and a TV screen providing the only light. "The hostage thing?"

He shook his head ruefully as the screen showed a remote from the midtown brownstone where he had apparently spent the first part of the evening. "Your average garbage man going nuts because he was suspended. So, he shoots his wife and son and the patrolman called to the scene." He took a stride over to the set and hit the Power button. "Yesterday's news."

"For you."

He looked back at me without any side glances around the living room. "I'm off until two tomorrow," he said. "I'd like to take a drive and I'd like you to come along. We can exchange notes on the way."

The trickle was back in my intestines. "Stanton?"

"Not that I know about. But I'd like to talk to her and look over a few things up there."

"You're talking four, four-and-a-half hours each way!"

"I told you, I have until two tomorrow."

What persuaded me to go for my coat? More than anything it might have been that he had stood there for a good two minutes without a single survey of my place. There had been me, the TV set that had threatened to distract him, and me again. In all my years of entering new apartments and houses as a cop, I had maintained focus like that only twice, and both times I had been let in by a suspected shooter. Considering that he had just come from what seemed to have been a nasty siege, his single-mindedness about me had to buy him more than a gripe about how weary I was.

He had already gassed up his Accord and had two coffees waiting in the front seat. It took me about two blocks to real-ize he didn't intend taking four hours to reach Boston, that the gas pedal was going to have to put up with every one of his 280 pounds most of the way.

"We're being informal here, you understand," he said.

"Sure. On your off-hours. And why take the chance of being seen catching the shuttle at LaGuardia?"

He made a sound in his throat, then turned up the radio. The news announcer was talking about the Sanitation Depart-ment employee who had shot his wife, 10-year-old, and a cop. An eight-year-old girl might have joined the casualties, according to the announcer, if not for "the heroic gamble of Sergeant Dana McGill." Bernstein snapped off the radio before I could hear what McGill had done.

"Played the moron, that's what. Almost got herself killed."

"But you'll take her."

"Fucking right. But tell her that. As far as she's concerned, I'm just patronizing her. Sometimes I think she has a point."

"What's yours?"

He looked disappointed he couldn't wax further about McGill. He took a deep breath to remind himself he was the one who had invited me along. "Something Vincent said at our last confab. He was talking about Stanton. A couple of things I guess you know."

"Like what?"

"Like her allegiances to her own sex."

"Are you serious?"

"I'm giving you a cinder track, Finley. Inch ahead a little."

"It's late."

"What I was thinking was, if I had real true-blood Americans out there, honest taxpayers who sent their kids to school with an extra quarter for the United Way canister and who watched the Jets religiously every Sunday, if I had these real apple pie Americans out there and I had a hunch they were in danger because of something they had no control over, boy, I'd move my ass to make sure they had the Bureau's full protection."

I saw where he was going. "But if they weren't such solid citizens?"

"Just for the sake of argument, of course. We all know FBI recruiters are out there beating the bushes for every gay black with a Chinese mother they can find so they can show the world the Hoover Era is ancient history. But that odd old-timer who hasn't been pensioned off yet? Some of those hard-to-get-at dust balls in the Bureau's broom closets? Excuse me for even thinking it, but if patriots like that thought they could net some very bad guys with the help of a gay storekeeper and this guy who's given them some bad hours on Long Island . . . well, why *not* dangle them? The worst that can happen is . . . the worst that can happen."

"Lovely."

"Just a thought."

"But enough of one for this little ride?"

He took 27 to connect with the Van Wyck. "It took me a long time to figure out who to call in Boston, Finley. And even he's nervous. Wants me to do all the talking to Stanton because it's not going to be his neck when Vincent finds out he's lost his sitting duck. Me, I need you to help me convince her."

It was as good an opening as any for telling him about Lerico. He was as confused as I was. "That doesn't make any goddamn sense!"

"Somewhere it does."

"That and a MetroCard gets you on the subway."

"Do I believe Lerico? Why shouldn't I? He could've sent me off with Paz and Miranda like that!"

"What're you saying?"

The idea had been clearer before I had started watching all the sitcoms. "There's more teams on the field than we thought," I tried anyway. "Paz represents Team A—the visitors. The ambassador Montaldo represents Team B—the home club. Now, is Lerico talking for Team B or does he represent Team C? And what about his boss Becquer?"

Bernstein thought about it while he negotiated a cigar wrapper around the steering wheel. "Mind if I ask where you got all these insights?"

"Team Q, maybe."

He waited for more, then realized there wasn't going to be any. "So what do you figure?" he asked, pulling a lighter out of his blanket of a coat. "The Mets in it this year?"

"Middle of the pack."

He went back to the white line of the thruway. Near Norwalk, he told me about his conversation with Ortega. "If he stammers in the classroom like he did with me, those classes must go on forever. I told him to regard himself as a material witness and to be careful one of those *60 Minutes* guys didn't come knocking at his door to ask a lot of embarrassing questions. He didn't think I was funny."

Neither did I. Phil Ortega had been last year's laugh.

* * *

We were too late. Two blocks away I saw the squad cars blocking the mouth of the cul-de-sac. Most of the lights were out in the Wooden Quarter, but there were still people drifting around inside near the bar and front booths. I assumed they were cops.

Bernstein said something, but I didn't hear it. I wanted it to be official. Not just probable because of the patrol cars. Not just semi-official because of the EMS attendants. Not just all-but-announced because of the bartender staring out from the Wooden Quarter's darkened window at the High Note. I waited for Bernstein to call out to a chunky plainclothes with wisps of red hair and for the plainclothes to amble over to the car window and say it: "Rosemary Stanton. Shot twice in the head."

It was official.

Bernstein hadn't thrown out the coffee containers and had topped my cigarette butts in the ashtray with two cigar butts. I opened my door, dropped the cups into the gutter, and emptied the ashtray over them. He kept muttering to the plainclothes, whose name was Caruso. I suddenly became "Sergeant Dan Mc-Gill." When I looked back at them, Caruso was nodding to me as a colleague and Bernstein was glaring at me with a warning not to complicate his life further. I didn't: Sergeant Dan McGill put back the ashtray and got out of the car. I didn't care what lies they were telling one another. I just didn't want to be near them.

The coffee and cigarettes had given my throat and bronchi a good workout; the cold air felt like one more rasp being denied. Looking down the dead-end street, I tried to recreate the sounds of the cello, but they didn't have a chance against the tall inspector who was shouting for a blue to do something, against the parade of black bags coming out of the High Note, and against the spinning roof lights all the way down to the garage. Had she had time to take Norma Fruchter's name off the front door? I hoped so. If she had, it might have meant she hadn't forgotten about me as soon as we had said goodbye.

"I'm going to take a look."

Bernstein kept his eyes averted to button his coat, and I knew it wasn't to locate the buttons. "I'll wait here."

It was the answer he wanted, and he immediately waded into the patrol cars after Caruso toward the store. My fingers clawed into piles of change in my pocket. I hated buying cigarettes from gouging vending machines, but I had a feeling we'd be back on the road to New York as soon as Bernstein had seen what he wanted to see and the machine was right next to the door of the Wooden Quarter. A plainclothes gave me a long look as I walked in but then went back to question one of the skels I'd seen in the bar on my first trip. I must have looked like a Sergeant Dan McGill.

I started feeding quarters into the slot, surprised that coin machines for cigarettes still existed and that I had accumulated

enough change to sell papers on the corner. I had the Panamanian Balboa halfway in before I grabbed it back. Having it bothered
me again, and this time I put it in an empty pocket to make sure
I gave it to Bernstein. I hadn't given him the coin from the Hotel
Vega, he hadn't called the 718 area code in Queens to find Hector Miranda, and Vincent hadn't put anyone on Rosemary. No, it
didn't even up; I still felt ahead on points.

I stood outside the bar smoking, mainly to tell my chest to
fuck itself.

Who the hell *was* Rosemary Stanton?

Somebody out of bounds for me in the sex game so somebody
I couldn't have bullshitted even if I had wanted to.

That didn't seem like much of a headstone afterthought.

But neither did Manuel Lerico, and that was what was rising
in my throat with the tar and nicotine. But if not Lerico, who? His
boss Becquer? Had Lerico suddenly found religion, gotten uneasy
about the purification mission he and Becquer were on? It was
possible, but so were cows with six feet. Nearing had called Lerico
a thug, and when I wasn't being grateful he hadn't dispatched
me in my elevator, I had to admit he looked like exactly that. And
thugs didn't just get uneasy.

Bernstein finally emerged from the High Note with Caruso.
They stood exchanging professional courtesies for a minute, then
the fat man started back through the maze of fenders to his car.
"Back to New York?"

"Short stop first," he said, keying the engine before I closed
my door.

I didn't ask for details on what he had seen, and he didn't vol-
unteer them. Our destination was an office building on Marlbor-
ough that he found with Caruso's directions. I stayed put in the
car as he rang a night bell, waited for a watchman, then flashed
his badge to get inside. Five minutes later he came out again. By
then I'd figured out where he had gone. "Feds?"

He was suddenly meticulous about wrapping his seatbelt
around his big stomach, as though hoping to come up with another reason for staying in Boston. "I asked for Vincent. They
said they haven't heard from him in weeks. I asked who was on

the Stanton surveillance. They looked at me like I had two heads. Those clicks you hear right now are the phones on the fifth floor racking up message units."

"Was that wise?"

"I'm steering blind here, Finley! Splashing a little water! You got a better idea for me?"

I didn't.

* * *

At least until we were back on the turnpike. "Did it ever occur to you, Bernie, that you have one piece of evidence you shouldn't?"

It hadn't.

"I mean the address book."

"What about it?"

"Well, take the popular theory—Paz came here for Montaldo."

"Yeah?"

"Becquer and Lerico beat Paz to the punch," I said, piecing it out for myself as much as for him. "And then they start going after all these so-called contacts Paz was supposed to have here."

"Oh, Jesus!" It was practically a moan. "*So why leave the goddamn book there in the room!!??*"

"Of course the shooter could've been in a hurry," I said, refusing to believe what suddenly seemed so obvious.

"Not this shooter. Not in a swamp like the Vega."

"What I was thinking."

"That son of a bitch Vincent's been giving us a bum steer all along!"

I remembered Nearing's certainty. "No, I don't think so."

"Why not? Now you believe Vincent about that but nothing else?"

"Vincent isn't the only one pushing the assassination theory."

The fat man didn't need his patience tested any further. "It'd be a real treat for me, Finley, if I knew where you were getting all this stuff."

"I'd tell you if I could. But I think it's genuine."

"Fine. You can sit on it at the Ramada Inn."

"What're you talking about?"

"You don't think you're dancing back to your apartment, do you? I don't care how much you've fallen in love with Lerico. He didn't have too much clout with whoever did Stanton."

He was right, of course; depressingly right. And I might have sunk back into my futile speculations if I hadn't caught the lights bearing down on Bernstein's rearview mirror. There wasn't another car within half a mile ahead or behind. I told myself the driver was one of the Boston FBI agents Bernstein had just rattled, determined now to get to Vincent in New York before we did.

That was the fancy; the reality was a dark Toyota that wasn't using the free middle lane to get past us.

"He's been hanging back there a long time," Bernstein said.

"Go right. See if he passes."

"Jesus, there's an idea! Pick that up on the Island?"

The sarcasm only emphasized the break in his voice. He moved right, and I checked my seatbelt. By the time I looked up again, I told myself, the Toyota would be passing on the left.

I was half-right. It brought its headlights up to our tail. I made out two men; neither was Lerico or anyone else I knew. Wasn't it too good to be true they were coming right out to be seen? Yes, it was. The passenger in the front suddenly lowered his window and hit me in the eyes with some kind of nuclear-powered spotlight. The last thing I saw clearly was that the light nozzle was a good three or four times broader than the handle. My vision turned to blotches of green-blue amoebas. I thought Bernstein gave me a look. I heard his curse, felt his desperate acceleration.

"It's souped-up, Bernie!"

I suppose if I had been on the Dodger bench after Bobby Thomson had tagged Ralph Branca's second pitch in the 1951 playoffs, I would have jumped up and screamed: "It's a home run!" For sure, Bernstein didn't need my play-by-play. The Toyota gained on him yards at a time. We both knew what the light man was up to—and it didn't matter we knew because we were going to crash anyway. Bernstein tried moving all the way to the right, over to the guardrail, but the Toyota stayed a yard or two ahead of him, just enough to let the light man keep his glares focused on the wheel. Moving over to the guardrail had been stupid, of course; what Bernstein should have done was stay in the center lane where the worst obstacle would have been a dead squirrel. I made a note to tell him that in the next world.

He tried slowing down and stopping, but the Toyota was having none of it. Its back fender came into us with a thwack. He tried to get his foot off the brake, but his brown Oxford reacted milliseconds too slowly. I wanted to believe he was swerving deliberately, that he was working on some ingenious counter-ploy that hadn't dawned on me. But even I knew it couldn't have included the top bar of the guardrail suddenly ahead of us. The rusted piece of iron had been torn from its bolsters and was lying lazily over the asphalt patch between the guard line and a strip of grassy dirt. He couldn't have hit it more squarely if he had aimed at it.

That historical review people are supposed to experience in their final seconds? What mainly flashed before my eyes was a souped-up black Toyota finally leaving us some space on the turnpike as it shot off to become merely tail lights. There was black lettering on the guardrail, a tree trunk that looked like a face, and a pen in my shirt pocket that was pressing against my seatbelt. The traffic in both directions that hadn't been there while the Toyota had been doing its worst, that seemed to have returned a car at a time, too. And then there was all the rattling and shaking I was sure would have stopped if either I'd commanded it loudly enough or Bernstein stopped doing the wrong thing. It was almost a relief when he finally broadsided the second tree. At least my head stopped trying to get through the roof and my seatbelt subsided. I was alive: that much I knew at once. But I didn't know what the big deal was. Who wanted to live on a planet of binding seatbelts and grainy knees?

* * *

The next few hours were complicated. Bernstein had taken a big hit on his left shoulder, and I did a lot of dithering between trying to get his door over calf-high brambles and helping him across the front seat through the passenger door without destroying whatever tendons remained in the shoulder. I didn't take any of his swearing personally; I thought of it as directed against the dozens of cars that ripped past us without a second look. A salesman named Ambrose salvaged what was left of my naturally sunny outlook by pulling over, helping Bernstein into his Taurus, then using his cell phone to call the Highway Patrol. Ambrose taught me two things: that cell phones had their moments and that we were no longer in Massachusetts, but in Rhode Island.

The Highway Patrol showed up in the person of Stick and Stick II—two guys who seemed to have been shoved into their Smokey the Bear hats and knee-high boots after finishing their basketball careers. Bernstein had only to hear their leading questions to trot out all the snarling I'd been treated to while squeezing him out of his car. By design or not, the snarling worked: The questions stopped and Stick II agreed to stay by the car while Stick drove us to a hospital about three miles away. A blond doctor with an afternoon soap opera in his future gave me a once-over, concluding I needed nothing more than a tea from a vending machine in the lobby. He ingratiated himself to Bernstein forever by, first, making him sit by on an Emergency Room table while he poked at me and, then, turning to him and blithely announcing: "I'd say broken collarbone. How do you feel about X-rays?"

I left Dr. Kildare to his punishment and settled down in the lobby with a tea, as instructed. Stick spoiled it with a lot of predictable questions about the crash. I hadn't had the chance to clear it with Bernstein, but I left out the parts about the glare light and the Toyota's decisive bump into the rail. As it turned out, Bernstein was leaving out the same parts in his tale to the doctor. But what I hadn't anticipated, when he came out an hour later with his left arm encased in a sling, was what he told McGill by phone. With Stick hovering a few feet away, he told her not even to think about coming all the way up to Rhode Island, but to pick us up instead at Port Chester. Then he hung up and, before Stick could lay out the prospects for an escort down to Westchester, he picked up the reception desk phone again in search of a listing in Mystic. The next thing I knew, he was talking to some friend on the force in Connecticut and asking him to give us a ride from Mystic to Port Chester. Stick looked happy he wasn't going to have to find somebody to do the honors all the way to the New York state line and went outside to make a call on his car radio.

"Nothing like getting every cop on the East Coast in on this."

Bernstein grinned. "Should really piss off Vincent, don't you think?"

I got it. Before I could return his smile, though, he was wincing from his first stupid attempt to move his left arm.

* * *

It was while we were sitting in the back of the car of a Mystic robbery detective named Jack Fine that I remembered the coin from the Vega. Bernstein weighed it in his good hand, giving half an ear to some Fine story about some gang that specialized in pawn shops.

"Probably Paz's," I said. "Mr. and Mrs. Rabbit wouldn't let anything stay on the floor too long."

"You mean I should charge *them* with withholding evidence?"

"If you feel up to it."

He dropped the Balboa in his shirt pocket. "Fuck you."

Jack Fine looked around at us wondering what he had missed. At that point, I still didn't know.

FIVE

Living in a hotel in your own city is disorienting. On the one hand, you feel like you've been sent to the sidelines during a game only you can win; you want to shriek at every deskman, guest, and coffee shop waitress that you belong out there as much as they do. On the other hand, when you get taken in by the hall ice machines and the elevator Muzak, you feel like strolling out to see the Grand Canyon, only to end up face to face with some dreary stretch of the LIE.

There had been no arguing with Bernstein. As soon as McGill had reached the city line, he had ordered her to the Ramada Inn. His notion of a concession had been to let me give McGill a list of things I needed from my apartment. The next morning, she showed up in my room with my biggest valise and a Key Food tote bag full of my work files. I hadn't liked the insinuations behind her choice of suitcases, and said so; her answer was that the Key Food bag had been "the handiest." I didn't believe her, and she didn't care in the least.

The house rules weren't the worst for a penitentiary. I could conduct business for Finley Investigations if I didn't say where I was living and didn't meet anybody near my apartment, the Professor's place, the university campus, or other places I was known to frequent. Too bad for the kids, but they were going to have to get by "a week or so" without hearing about law enforcement's practical problems. Too bad for the Professor, but he was going to have to be satisfied with a quick phone call saying I'd be out of town for several days. It was a little disheartening having to admit nobody else had to be told anything.

Bernstein, McGill, and Masterson took turns visiting—usually in the evening. There was no fourth. Bernstein was playing me so close to the vest he hadn't shared my whereabouts with anybody else. Given the thrift in manpower around me, I wasn't all that surprised to discover that, along with too much underwear and not enough shirts, McGill had stuck my .38 in the valise. Evidently, I was expected to watch my own back most of the time. The bright side of that, of course, even granting it had probably been Bernstein's idea, was that it was a sign of how much McGill admired me.

As for where things were going, Bernstein dropped by the second night with some cryptic reassurances that "the message is making its way up to the right people." I didn't know what that meant, and he added nothing to clarify it. He also brought a copy of the *Boston Globe,* which said the police were investigating Rosemary Stanton's murder as a robbery gone wrong. Bernstein shrugged before I could explode, and I told myself that lie too would be avenged by the brilliant scheme the fat man was working on.

Whatever the hell it was.

By the fourth day of living under my ceiling for elves, I was getting seriously antsy. It wasn't that I hadn't run up a pretty good phone bill chasing down new clients and inventing excuses for lack of progress for the old ones; in fact, I devoted more than one down minute to calculating how I could get the NYPD to pay for my phone charges. Once Masterson had brought my car, I'd also been able to get down to City Hall to check out the licensing of a notary and to the 42nd Street library to look up accounts of a suspicious 1992 fire for another case. In short, my sense of isolation arose not from being cut off from humanity, but from being cut off from that part of humanity that didn't constantly remind me of my bank book or Victor Paz's telephone address book. All by way of saying that I massaged some of Bernstein's rules to call Angela Balestrini.

* * *

We met in an Italian restaurant in Hempstead that Angela rated "not bad." I'd assumed this meant the food was spectacular by any standards outside those of Rome and the La Boca district in Buenos Aires, but the stuffed mushrooms and veal pizzaiola turned out to be just that—"not bad." She wore a high-collared black wool dress, teardrop earrings, and a thin silver bracelet she fussed with whenever she didn't have her fork or wine glass in her hand. Her raven hair was the shoulder length I preferred to the bun she had worn the night of the university dinner for the Commerce Secretary, but I wasn't going to protest the Chanel she had gone back to from that evening. I wasn't going to protest anything. At first, I didn't even want to talk. I just wanted her to spill over everything the way she seemed ready to do. She was happy to be subletting the apartment of a political scientist who had gone off to Denmark on sabbatical and was getting down to the nitty-gritty of her research project on the role of American multinationals in Argentina's development. "I have to be finished by May," she smiled. "There will be no more money after that."

Because of a tacit pact to establish ourselves to each other as people interesting in our own right, we didn't mention the Ortegas until halfway through the meal. "I saw him on the campus yesterday," Angela said, "and I told him everything I should not have."

"Like what?"

"Like why he and Barbara have not called since I moved out."

"He said he was busy."

"And not very sincerely. What happened between you two?"

"He lied to me and I caught him at it."

She took it in with her wine. "You must be good at doing that. A policeman must have a second sense about lies, no?"

"It's got nothing to do with being a cop."

Somewhere on her plate, between her chicken and zucchini, she rediscovered a character flaw of mine she had apparently tried to set aside after some revelation at the Professor's. "Everybody lies and everybody gets caught in lies," she said carefully. "Is it always important to let people know you have caught them?"

"In this case, yes."

"And you will not forgive him?"

"It's something that happened, Angela," I said, hearing my impatience at the questions. "It's over."

"That's not what I asked."

"Let's just say this lie could have killed me."

"Because of Phil?"

"Good old Phil."

"I think you flatter him."

What had happened to the evening without the Paz address book? "Let's drop it, okay? All I can tell you is I'm not just talking about Phil Ortega the academic go-getter."

"But that *is* Phil Ortega."

I might have been talking to Nearing. "So everybody says."

"Don't get angry."

"I'm not angry," I said, becoming more so with every word. "But if you're talking about his ivory tower career, I'm not sure he's been all that harmless there, either."

"The things he says at the Professor's?"

"The word is hypocrisy."

She shook her head without hesitation. "No, it is his self-delusion. He is so powerful with some general so he does not have time for his Indio? He feels so much commiseration for his Indio—one, just one—that the generals will not trust him or practice what he proposes? You don't believe all that, do you?"

What I was beginning to believe was that the musticst library files didn't have a prayer against her relentlessness if she went at her research the way she was going at me. "The second part, no. The first part? He seems to use that dinner jacket a lot."

She seemed on the verge of guffawing. And why not? I had waded into waters she was more accustomed to than I was. "Yes. And he also gets to use academic journals, world conferences, and corporate executives who pay him to study their companies. And none of it means anything."

"That isn't the impression I've had over the years."

"Oh, yes. You mean the smart young technocrats in Latin America who say they admire the theories from Long Island and Chicago and Berkeley and want to implement them at home, no matter how many people they make miserable in the process."

"In school, we called it Current Events in the Banana Republics."

The guffaw finally came. "Except the first time they see the theories are not adapted so easily, these smart young technocrats discard them and go back to the important matter of protecting their positions. People like Phil have no theories of power, Paul. At most, they admire those who have the theories and act like cocks of the walk because they once met their hero at a dinner or banquet. Phil Ortega is a speechwriter. When speechwriters have the right connections, they are asked to submit a word or two, sometimes an entire phrase. It's their reward for their declaration of sympathy, for their willingness to close their eyes to what is unpleasant, even brutal. Only a self-deluded American—an arrogant self-deluded American—thinks he has more influence than that."

"I think I was talking about something more personal."

She found something funny at the end of her fork. "And saying that is none of my business. So, I can only speak about what remains—the historical, the sociological, the impersonal. I think that is very accommodating of me, don't you?"

"Is it that important to you to know?"

"Not now."

"Angela . . ."

She suddenly reached over and pressed her finger over my lips. "When the truth comes out sounding like resignation, it is another kind of lie," she said evenly. "I do not want you to lie to me. I am here only for a short time. We don't need lies, especially because of Phil Ortega."

So, we went back to talking about exotic things. Right: She might have been visiting, but I was the tourist.

I still felt that way in front of her apartment building four blocks away from the restaurant. "You have been uncomfortable all night," she said, taking out her key. "That is one reason I feel bad. The other is because it has less to do with me than I would like."

I thought of all the old new excuses. Jennifer, naturally. And then Ellen Miles going from protégé to partner to aggrieved representative of the Nassau gentry. And of course, Rosemary

Stanton—not just untouchably gay, but untouchably dead. "Sometimes I have them all in my head. All of them hurting and blaming me for it while I act like the one really hurt."

She didn't give an inch. "Maybe you *are* hurt. That doesn't have to be false. But maybe it also isn't important you are. Isn't that a possibility?"

She opened the street door and went into the fluorescent-lighted lobby. I caught the street door, then caught her before she could open the vestibule door. Her eyes were already closed when she turned her head around, and I imagined that the extra Chanel scent had come from some deep corner of her eyelids that she had finally consented to release over her face and both our bodies.

* * *

The bed table clock said 4:10 when I pulled it into my eyes. I managed to put it back without dislodging Angela's ankle, but it wasn't much of an achievement. "You cannot sleep, either?" she asked.

"You followed me into my dreams and I got excited again."

She shifted with a light snort of a laugh but ended up in the exact same position on her stomach. "You should be so lucky."

I should have been. What I shouldn't have been was back at the table in the restaurant. "You are still with that person's lies," she said for both of us. "I can feel it from here."

"One question?"

"If you must."

"You don't seem to respect him very much. How come you had no qualms about moving in with him and his wife?"

She pounded the sheet next to her face in mock agony. "I hear the famous purity critique again!"

"How come?"

It took forever under the twisted blanket, but she turned her body around to me. Her eyes peeked out in amusement from her wild hair. "He is a colleague who invited me," she said. "Getting the work done is what is important. Colleagues understand that. The rest is secondary."

"So if they went to Buenos Aires . . ."

"Yes, I'd have little choice."

"Spoken like a cynical Latin."

"*Portenos* are not cynical, only practical," she said, less amused.

"I seem to have heard that before."

"There is a saying in Lunfardo, our dialect. 'Nobody has earned enough detachment from the world to be cynical.' So, when you talk about the *portenos* of Buenos Aires, you are talking about people who are cynical only about those who would pride themselves on being cynical."

"Cutting out the middleman."

"I'm not sure that is what I'm saying. Americans always seem to like middlemen anyway. The more there are, the happier they are. It gives a role in the economy to everybody."

I laughed as she re-fixed her head on the pillow so that her eyes glistened from the lamppost outside the window; it felt more manly than saying I didn't know what the hell she was talking about. Coming right down to it, I was beginning to think we spoke entirely different languages, and neither English nor Spanish was in the equation. "What position did you take?" she asked, sounding like she had secured a wanted distance. "In your argument with Ortega. There is always a position, even on lies."

I moved up to kiss her dry lips awkwardly. She put the tip of her tongue out, but nothing else. "You're the pigeonholer. Guess."

"That is what disturbs me," she said. "The opposite position to Phil Ortega is . . . Phil Ortega."

A car went by in the street. It wasn't moving fast or recklessly enough to break her stare.

* * *

There was a message from Bernstein waiting for me at the hotel desk the next morning. Punching out his number in my room, I realized I wasn't calling his office. The area code was Manhattan, but the random numbers said he had a home somewhere. So did the radio behind him when he picked up. "McGill pack your formal wear?"

"Why?"

"Bolivian Embassy this afternoon at 3:30. Meet me at the zoo entrance to Central Park on Fifth at 3:15. Don't be late."

"What's going on?"

"I told you. Wear a suit and tie. Diplomats like that kind of thing."

"Vincent in on this?"

He laughed; mirthlessly. "More than he wants to be."

He hung up before I could ask anything else. But his tone said he had delivered on his promise to get the "message" to the right people. I saw two deportation orders for Becquer and Lerico coming up on rye.

The first worm hatched and began slithering around inside me just as I hit the 59th Street bridge that afternoon. Hiccoughing along behind a pickup truck advertising SAL'S TILES AND FIXTURES, I played over the part about the deportations. That was about all the Feds could do against people covered by diplomatic immunity, and it didn't seem like very much for what had happened to the Miranda family and Rosemary. But what about my doubts Lerico had been involved in those killings? What would have been gained by throwing him out of the country? Some moral vindication that he was a thug who had probably turned his share of thumbscrews in the past against other people? That past hadn't prevented the State Department from letting him in, to begin with, so what was the big deal now?

I found a parking space on 62nd Street below Madison and walked up to the park. Bernstein was sitting with Masterson on a Fifth Avenue bench near the zoo entrance. "Not bad," he said, taking in my charcoal suit, topcoat, and best off-white shirt.

That made one of us since his only concession to the formality of the day was a black silk sling; otherwise, he looked as stuffed into his three-piece gray suit as he had the first night we'd met. Masterson hadn't even gone that far: jeans, logger's boots, and a rabbit-collared coat. He also acted more interested in the llamas on the other side of the zoo wall than in any Bolivian diplomats and their security men.

"Am I supposed to have lines?"

"Very easy ones," Bernstein said. "You sit there and keep a zipper on it. You're the nuclear weapon—dangerous because of what you could do, not what you do do. Got it?"

"Vincent's script?"

"His superior, suit named Hyde. Hyde got a little exercised when he heard about the Boston cops and the Rhode Island cops and the Connecticut cops. Vincent should be there, but it's Hyde's show. That means it's not mine and it's not yours. Right?"

"Whatever you say."

He weighed my answer a long moment before turning to Masterson, who had stood to watch some kids petting a black-and-white goat. "Jimmy, you wait here till McGill comes. Anybody comes out of that embassy while we're inside, especially to that phone booth, I want to know the color of the socks he's wearing."

"Suppose the guy has a cell phone and doesn't need the booth?"

"Then he'll have a cell phone and not need the booth. But I still want to know the color of his socks."

Masterson took it in dimly. "No sweat."

Our destination was direct across the street, one building off Fifth, under Bolivia's green, yellow, and red flag. The pay phone Bernstein had pointed out was only a few yards from the entrance. Even if it worked, I couldn't imagine it not carrying the traps of every federal agency there was. A brass plate identified the sanded townhouse as the BOLIVIAN MISSION TO THE UNITED NATIONS. That was a rung below a full-fledged embassy, but the marble foyer wasn't a rung below anything.

An old man in a sleeveless yellow sweater looked at Bernstein's ID card without reading anything, then waved us after him to an oak door that had probably been shining since the 19th-century battle depicted on the wall painting next to it. Behind the door was a conference room with a table so enormous it barely left space for the dozen or so chairs around it. Vincent and Hyde were sitting in the middle across from each other. Vincent had two file folders in front of him, Hyde a single piece of paper. Military heroes with sailboat hats glowered down on them from every inch of wall.

The old man closed the door behind us, the catch of the lock forcing Hyde to acknowledge us. He was about 50, tall and balding, with skin that seemed to have been stripped from a reptile and tanned. I'd seen him on the news a few weeks before bragging about how his office had broken up a Brooklyn ATM gang. He looked as ill at ease now as he had then.

"You've been told your role here, Mr. Finley?"

I thought about taking Bernstein's warning literally, not answering the question. But Hyde didn't look like he would have appreciated a joke. "Whatever I can do to help."

Vincent strummed his fingers on the folders as if to say he had warned Hyde. Bernstein went over to Vincent's side of the table while I took a seat a couple of chairs up from Hyde. I was wondering about the smoking rules when a white door at the lower end of the room opened and a small parade came in. First up was a nervous, bouncy man with the look of a public relations flack. Behind him came the ambassador, Montaldo, who had gained a good 25 pounds since Nearing's photograph, all of them in the gut and face. That still left him a featherweight next to Becquer, who rolled as much as he walked and who was even more of an old tank in person than in Nearing's gallery. My buddy Lerico was low enough in the pecking order to have to close the door behind everybody.

Hyde hesitated about standing up but did. Vincent gave it a quick knee bend. I looked over at Bernstein, who was preoccupied resettling his arm more comfortably on the table. I wanted to see if he succeeded, so I ignored the curtsies, too.

Montaldo took the chair at the head of the lower end of the table, and Becquer and Lerico filled in the first two spaces to his left. The flack, who had come with an armful of folders in brown and purple shades I had never seen at Office Depot, deposited them in front of the seat to Montaldo's right but didn't sit. He cleared his throat deliberately, then singled out Hyde as his audience. "Ambassador Montaldo has reviewed all the documentation," he said in a squeaky voice. "Yours as well as our own. His government's position is that there are no grounds for requesting that either Senor Becquer or Senor Lerico leave the United States."

Score one for my deportation theory. Bernstein looked at me to see if I was surprised. I was more interested in the reaction of Hyde, who had apparently expected a rollover win because he had to nod to himself to accept the reality of what he had just been told. "My government also has a position," he said finally. "Mr. Finley?"

Hadn't I been told to keep my mouth shut? "What?"

Hyde pointed down the table. "Is Senor Lerico there the man you saw in Boston shortly before Rosemary Stanton was killed?"

I could have done without the "shortly before," but even Bernstein seemed to be rooting for the right answer. "He's the one."

The flack gave me a pained smile. "I'm sure Mr. Finley . . ."

Montaldo finally moved—with an arm slice that might have cost the flack his head if he had been standing any closer. "We do not deny Senor Lerico was in Boston, Mr. Hyde," he said, enunciating each word heavily. "Nor do we deny he was keeping this ill-fated woman under surveillance until he had an opportunity to speak with her. In this Senor Lerico was acting with considerable more zeal in a certain investigation than American agencies we could name."

I liked that: from one sleazeball to another. But Hyde hadn't come for a debate. "My agenda today is very specific, Mr. Ambassador," he said stiffly. "If you have complaints about an official body, I can help you forward them to the appropriate people. But for now, I am authorized only to extend the request that Senor Becquer and Senor Lerico leave the United States within 24 hours. Failure to comply with our request will necessitate a formal order to the same effect."

Lerico, who had been hidden from me by Hyde's shoulder, suddenly hung out over the table. If the fury in his eyes hadn't been so democratic, I might have thought he was blaming me for everything. "We have done nothing unlawful! Absolutely nothing!"

"You don't deny being outside Ms. Stanton's store?"

"The ambassador has already answered that."

"Do you deny knowing Victor Paz was coming here with the explicit assignment of trying to assassinate Ambassador Montaldo?"

Montaldo winced and the flack looked outraged that his sense of protocol was being trampled by an interrogation. Lerico's face retreated behind Hyde's shoulder. There was only silence for a long moment. "We grant such a conspiracy has yet to be fully established," Hyde said, his point made. "And even as a mere possibility, Mr. Ambassador, be assured we take it very seriously. But there are sufficient indications suggesting your security people have been overzealous in defending against this threat."

Vincent was impressed by Hyde's delayed comeback, and Hyde's neck quivered with what I presumed was self-satisfaction. Montaldo looked more skeptical. "And if we accept this informal invitation of yours," he asked, "who will guarantee my security until replacements for Mr. Becquer and Mr. Lerico arrive? You, Mr. Hyde?"

"Fly in two more people."

Montaldo didn't know whether to laugh or spit. "And we could count on all the necessary clearances being completed in 24 hours?"

Vincent didn't like sarcasm. "We can't help it if you have a problem undergoing quick security checks . . ."

I knew the second twitch from Hyde's neck wasn't self-satisfaction. "Leave it, Frank. As to your question, Mr. Ambassador, yes, we can provide enough protection until your replacements arrive. Within our jurisdiction, of course. We aren't employees of your government."

Montaldo wasn't buying, and as soon as the flack saw his expression, he wasn't, either. "That's too vague, Mr. Hyde."

Hyde shrugged and picked up the sheet in front of him; he fluttered it comically in the air. "The replacement matter can be resolved. But that is a separate matter, and I still have my instructions not to leave today without your reply to the departure request."

I figured that was an opening for Becquer finally to join the friendly conversation, but he kept sitting stolidly in all his chins until Montaldo got to his feet. "In the interests of maintaining the friendly relations between our countries," the diplomat said, "we do not appear to have much choice. Senor Becquer and Senor

Lerico will be on a flight to La Paz tomorrow morning. Will that be adequate?"

Hyde couldn't get up fast enough. "Thank you, sir."

How many things were wrong? I stopped counting after Rosemary, Miranda, Miranda's relatives, and the black Toyota. Bernstein had been right to caution me on my manners because I had a sudden urge to go bowling down the table and grab one of the fat necks getting ready to go back through the white door. But I kept quiet.

Until Montaldo gave me a little bow from behind his chair. "I understand you have been involved in some of this unpleasantness, Mr. Finley. I'm sure the worst has passed for you now."

"That puts me up on some people."

Hyde took too long to turn around to me, so Vincent got it in first. "We'll talk outside, Finley."

"Fuck you, Frank. And your friend here, too."

Magic words for Montaldo: He immediately raised his hand to stop the flack's nudging toward the white door. "Something you would like to say, Mr. Finley?"

"Only the obvious. You have to admit you're getting off pretty cheap for all the bodies left around."

He was the latest to think I was amusing. "You think so?"

"I think so. When you clear all the talk out of this room, we still have two suspects in multiple homicides flying home."

Montaldo seemed to be getting more entertained by the second. "Oh, it's much more than that, Mr. Finley," he said. "Now we also have an emissary of the Republic of Bolivia entrusting his security to Mr. Hyde and Mr. Vincent here. I suspect everything else has been irrelevant. Good Day."

I had no answer to that—or to Lerico's glance before he trailed the others through the door. The thug looked as if I had betrayed him!

"That wasn't helpful, Finley," Hyde said. "In case you haven't realized it, you've been out of danger from the second you walked in here. Tell him, Lieutenant."

Bernstein sat tapping his cast absently. He had seen everything and heard everything, and now needed practice to be able to talk again after so much silence. Finally, as Hyde and Vincent raced each other out of the room in a huff, he acknowledged he was still there with me. "He's right. No reason you can't go back to your apartment."

I watched Hyde and Vincent pass the old man with the yellow sweater in the foyer and get to the front door. I knew I had just been traded, but I didn't have the slightest idea for whom.

* * *

Bernstein kept his own counsel until we were back across Fifth Avenue to the benches outside the zoo. Masterson had left; in his place was McGill, looking like a bundled-up mother waiting for her kids to get bored with the animals and return to her.

"There's still a big piece missing," Bernstein grumbled by way of greeting her. I didn't know where he got that from; I counted about a hundred pieces missing.

"Had a thought," McGill said.

"Is it worth anything?"

She took off a blue mitten and reached into her bomber jacket. I don't know why I didn't moan when she came out with my Panamanian coin, but I felt close to it. "About a quarter," she said. "And I was thinking that beautiful couple down at the Vega wouldn't have missed it if it'd been laying there more than a couple of days."

"Finley's had the same inspiration."

She had a chance to show me more admiration but preferred staring at the Balboa. "So let's assume it belonged to Paz."

"Yeah? So? He stopped off in Panama on his way here."

She shook her head. "Only places down there we know he was are the sailing point Caracas and Vera Cruz, the stop-off before here."

Bernstein looked ready to see what Masterson had found so interesting about the llamas. "So another trip. The one before this one."

McGill nodded, but it wasn't a concession; more like a confirmation of objections she had already posed to herself. "Then the timetable's all wrong, Bernie. He saw this teacher Ortega in

Bogota after Christmas. The freighter didn't make another trip up here since. I checked that."

Bernstein looked at me as though I should have understood faster than he did, but I couldn't help him. The only thing I understood was that McGill seemed to have worked out something that was going to make me feel like even more of an ass for keeping the coin so long.

"But even putting all that aside, there's something else."

"I wish you'd get to it, Mac."

"Lots of people around the world carry nickels and dimes in their pockets," she shrugged. "But wouldn't you bet ninety percent of them are Americans?"

I blamed my slowness on Ramada Inn living. I heard her. I had an image of Victor Paz strolling around Panama City and falling into the canal. And I still didn't know what I was supposed to be seeing. That was when Bernstein suddenly began shouting up and down Fifth Avenue. "No way! No way, Mac! No fucking way!"

McGill consulted the coin again. "It was Vincent who checked out the passport for us," she said, far too calmly.

My obtuseness finally cracked. "Victor Paz isn't Victor Paz!!??"

"That's the piece," Bernstein cried, "that's the fucking piece!"

An ancient rail of a man in a wheelchair and his nurse on the next bench looked scandalized by the outburst. I agreed with them. Bernstein was supposed to get that excited only when he drove into a tree.

"Where did you park, Mac?"

"Practically on Lexington."

Bernstein was having none of it. He yanked his body, sling first, off the bench and hurried out into the Fifth Avenue traffic. McGill and I were more tentative about two buses than he was. By the time we got to the phone booth, he had already been put through to somebody. McGill flashed him her cell phone uselessly. "It's the newest thing, Bernie! You don't need to run in front of buses and dig for quarters!"

He waved her quiet. " . . . That's right, Solly—Victor Paz. His prints. You didn't give them to your kids for a toy, did you? . . . Good to hear. What I need right now, this very second, is for you to send a copy of those prints to . . ."

"Panama City," McGill prompted.

"Panama City, Solly. It's in Panama . . . Glad your tuition wasn't wasted. Just get those prints off for a match . . . How the hell should I know? You got a directory there. Look it up. There's always some kind of Chen-trolley Regis-tray-o in those places . . . I need it yesterday. Which means you got a half-hour before I get there . . . Right."

Bernstein slammed down the receiver and was immediately out of impulses. A second later he wasn't too sure about the ones he had already vented. "Would the Feds fuck with us that much, Finley?"

I said the only thing that came to mind. "Depends on what they want and how bad they want it."

He had known that, had just wanted somebody else to say it. "Okay, we're going downtown. I wasn't bullshitting before. You can go home."

"Why? Because Hyde and Montaldo say so?"

"Because I said so. Because . . . All right, I *don't* know. I thought I had it figured, now I'm not sure. Maybe the hotel is still your best bet."

The Balboa was snug in one of McGill's pockets, but I could also feel it in mine when I had been talking to Hector Miranda on the phone, when I had been driving to Boston, and when I had been eating dumplings on the floor of the High Note. "I've got to know too, Bernie."

He wasn't ready to argue, especially with McGill already beginning to wander east toward her car. "All right. Follow us down."

It sounded like a reprieve of some sort.

* * *

Every time I hit a light going downtown I felt like running up the trunk of the car in front of me. The pieces were scattered around in my brain waiting for the simplest instructions to meld with one another. I didn't want them to meld, not yet, not until Solly had come up with the confirmation I was sure he was going to get from Panama City. Had it really been me who had been so indignant about Bernstein not tracing Miranda's phone number to Queens? If I had turned over that coin sooner, maybe all the

Mirandas, not to mention Rosemary, would still be alive. The guilt I had shared with the Professor for so long about Jennifer and Susan suddenly seemed to have been only Chapter One.

The desk sergeant had been told to expect me and pointed down a corridor smelling of linoleum. I knocked once on the computer room door and walked into a pastel space of wall-to-wall terminals. Bernstein and McGill were hovering over an operator in the far corner. McGill had taken off her jacket and thrown it on a high stool in the middle of the floor. The jacket struck me as some final sentinel warning me not to come any closer to see what I didn't want to see.

The operator, whom I took to be Solly, was clacking away at the keyboard. Bernstein didn't take his eyes off the monitor. McGill was kneading something in her pants pocket I took to be the Balboa. "It's got to be," Bernstein was muttering. "Just got to be."

Solly had a laugh like a hyena. "You sound like me at Belmont."

The monitor went dark for a second, then came back spitting lines like a Slinky falling down a staircase. The stamp-sized photo in the upper left-hand corner was as good as Victor Paz was ever going to look under the circumstances, I thought.

Except it wasn't a picture of Victor Paz.

"Jaime Olmos, Panamanian national," Solly read.

"Occupation seaman," McGill said over his shoulder.

Solly looked up at Bernstein. "Who's Jaime Olmos?"

The fat man kept his composure as he read the screen. "Somebody who wanted to make a quick buck, probably," he said, reaching for a cigar in his jacket pocket. "Thank Panama City and make me a copy of that."

Bernstein gave McGill's jacket on the stool a hard shove and hurried out. I went after him but didn't say anything until he was back in his office. "They ever fill your spot out in Mineola?" he asked, flopping behind his desk. "Maybe I can get a job there."

"You said it was your last piece. How?"

He winced before my idea of priorities, then struck a match for his cigar. "You were there. Montaldo didn't feel too secure without Becquer and Lerico. What did he say? That was the idea all along?"

"Yeah."

"That's what Lerico was warning you about in your elevator," he said, satisfied with his first puff. "If something happened to you or Stanton, the Feds had all the excuse they needed to bounce him and Becquer out."

"They already had that excuse with Miranda."

"Wake up and smell the coffee, Finley. You and Stanton weren't breadbasket America so, yeah, stake the two of you out. But in your worst days, you've never been an immigrant named Miranda in Jackson Heights. Even ex-cops have legs. And the gypsy cab driver versus the Irish lady in Boston with special sexual tastes? Which angle you think would have kept the front pages interested?"

I thought about telling him about Angela's saying about having to earn his cynicism, but knew it wouldn't have mattered. Besides, maybe he *had* earned it.

McGill came in with the printout and laid it on the desk. I hadn't noticed before there were reindeer on her sweater. "We can't assume it's just us and Panama City that know about our request," she said.

He nodded heavily. "Want to come to Mineola with me?"

She didn't mind showing me a corner of her tight smile. "What do I say to Vincent when he calls and you're not in?"

"Say 'it's all Finley's fault.' He's already stewing about his coin. Let's make him happy and crucify him all the way."

"If I'd known . . ."

He waved me quiet for a closer study of the printout on Jaime Olmos. McGill went to her window position and put her foot on the radiator. "The wonder of it is we've fucked up in so many directions and still have jobs," he said. "I played right into their hands with all that brouhaha in getting Rhode Island and Connecticut involved."

"Aren't we forgetting something?"

"What's that, Finley?"

"Victor Paz, the real Victor Paz, is still alive. And probably still coming here for Montaldo."

"Yeah, there's that."

"How do we even know there *is* a real Paz?" McGill objected.

"Because somebody you and I know, Mac, has a private channel of information that says there is. That right, private channel?"

I had to hold on to something even if it was only Nearing. "Paz knew Becquer and Lerico were waiting for him, so he tries to divert them with this Olmos. Who's Olmos? Like you said, probably just someone trying to save enough balboas to put a down payment on a car or house. Olmos thinks it's easy money for doing nothing except . . . what? Delivering an empty package to somebody at the Vega. That's probably why he had the duffel bag. But any pretext at all. Just as long as Olmos enters the country and registers at the Vega as Paz. You had that pegged from the start, Bernie. He was told to go there."

Bernstein wasn't in the mood for consolation prizes. "Swell. And the real Paz is here and he'll go after Montaldo and all the rest. And so what? What do I do with these profound conclusions? I bring them down the hall, calls get made, and then Hyde's accusing me of subverting the United States of America. And maybe I would be, at that."

"Hyde says a lot of shit."

"Oh, listen to him, Mac. He's out a few days of chasing philandering husbands while I've got 23 years of pension in the pot! Well, no thanks. I'm on the record. Something happens to Montaldo, even right here in front of this desk, I've got the paper to cover it. And we're not exactly talking about the Freedom Fighter of the Year here. You saw the guy. He learned to hold his temper only because goons like Becquer and Lerico can lose it for him. Know something, Finley? If you add it all up, we did okay. We screwed up left, right, and center, but we did okay!"

I looked over at McGill. For once she was staring at me instead of through me. It was how Ellen Miles had once waited for me to say what was on both our minds. Only now there seemed to be three of us waiting.

"What're you asking me to do, Bernie?"

Bernstein had the tact to drop his eyes to his sling and readjust the silk closer to his elbow. "All you have invested are some near-death experiences. Happens to anybody crossing Third Avenue."

"What?"

"If you insist, maybe there is one thing. It'd be nice to know how far certain people will go to protect their little operation. This still started off as my investigation and I'd get really pissed off if some people thought they could turn this command into Dallas. Maybe this source of yours . . . No, no. No names. Your secret."

"What exactly am I supposed to be listening for?"

He smiled. "I think you'll know when you hear it."

It wasn't only the prospect of another talk with Roger Nearing that felt like an anvil on my head. "I don't know what I hear anymore."

He didn't have time for that. "Everything gets sorted out in time."

"Really think so?"

"I'm not saying it gets sorted out and everybody lives happily ever after. I'm just saying it gets sorted out."

"But we must be quick," McGill said. "Becquer and Lerico leave tomorrow. Montaldo's never going to be as vulnerable as he will be over the next few days. We have to keep that in mind."

She didn't apologize for the *we* and I didn't feel like apologizing to Montaldo for having to take my place in Victor Paz's sights.

SIX

I hadn't expected Nearing to be enthusiastic about seeing me again, but he sounded as though he had been waiting for my call. The next morning at the same McDonald's? Good idea.

Right: Whenever I passed a mirror that day, I looked for the strings on my back. But since I couldn't do much about that so late in the game, I focused on getting re-accustomed to my apartment after the Ramada Inn Years. Aside from the thickened smell from the hamper, the major items waiting for me were a tape-load of phone messages and a hill of junk mail. Most of the calls were from that odd creature who spends his quarter listening to a taped message to the end, then hangs up when it's his turn to speak. One that wasn't was from Patrick Hardy. "An awful lot of people make dirty money, Finley," the Woodside druggist started off, "but you take the cake. You think you're helpin' anyone by ruinin' a man such as myself? You're a sorry excuse for a man, and with an Irish name at that. It wouldn't be you're really called Schwartz, would it?"

In a perfect world, I thought, Morgan and his phantom board of advisors would get 20 years for slandering Mrs. Morgan and Hardy would get off with a slap on the wrist for being such a donkey; but since it wasn't a perfect world, giving Hardy the 20 years would just have to do.

I didn't get around to the mail until I was about to turn in for the night. Yawning away on the couch, I was estimating the overall amount of money owed by the bills on the coffee table when I noticed the Air Mail edging on an envelope in the middle. Some muscle sank in my chest when I saw Rosemary Stanton's address. It was progress of some macabre kind: Paz had greeted me over someone else's body, but Rosemary was saying hello from over her own.

It was a note, written in a tight but squiggly hand using an off-brown color of ink. It said: *Dear Paul, This morning I took Norma's name off the door. Nothing has vanished except the letters, and they hadn't been for me anyway. The door still works, and so do I. All the best, Rosemary.*

I kept reading the note until I nodded off.

* * *

I got to McDonald's first. I bought a coffee and took the window seat next to the one we had used the first time. Nearing came in about five minutes later, blowing into his hands and rubbing them against the brisk morning. He reeked of lemon and lime cologne.

"Wish I hadn't already used up my coffee allowance for the morning," he said, breathing as if he had crossed an Arctic tundra.

"Increase the allowance."

"Once you start, you never stop. That's the secret to a lot of things. No one ever tell you that?"

He was so much cockier I sensed Team Q had risen in the standings since our last meeting. I also had a feeling I'd contributed to its rally.

"So how can I help you this time, Joe Carroll's son-in-law?"

"We had a sit-down yesterday at the Bolivian mission."

"That must've been interesting."

"Am I wasting my breath here, telling you what you know?"

"No, no," he said innocently. "Go ahead."

I wasn't convinced but plunged ahead anyway. He listened like a jaded priest duty-bound to look interested in boring sins.

"So how can I help you?" he asked as soon as I shut up.

"First question: Is there a real Victor Paz?"

No hesitation. "Yes."

"Is he here already?"

"Ask Immigration."

"If you had to take a wild guess."

"I don't take wild guesses. Figure it out yourself."

"All right, so let's say he's here and he's been very busy lately."

"Logical."

It was like being on the test range as a rookie cop: The further in I went, the more I could only screw up what I had already accomplished. "The way I see it, someone here has an interest in seeing a new government in La Paz. First target: Montaldo, the great statesman abroad. But since everybody in the Americas seemed to know Paz was coming after him, the defenses had to be lowered. So, this asshole Jaime Olmos was set up as a decoy. Becquer and Lerico bit, but . . ."

He looked positively entertained. "But what?"

"No, that's what it was *supposed* to look like. It wasn't Becquer and Lerico who did Olmos, it was the real Paz, who was already waiting here. And it was also Paz who blew up the Miranda house."

"Logical," he nodded again.

There was rockier road ahead. "But neither of those hits was enough. The media was blacked out on everything, so there was no real pressure the FBI could use to get Becquer and Lerico out of the country. That happened only when Paz went after Stanton."

"Don't underrate yourself and Bernstein," he said nonchalantly. "The Boston papers have treated Stanton's death the way the New York media has handled Olmos and the Mirandas. The real pressure came with the big ado about your little episode on the turnpike. Too many ears there."

"That's what Bernstein said."

"Good. So, what are you asking me?"

Suddenly, I wasn't so sure. There had been too much talk. Everybody knew everything and nobody did anything, but they all kept talking.

Except for one person, anyway.

"Wait a minute. At the mission yesterday, there was a mute in the crowd. Never opened his mouth."

Nearing was delighted with me. "Who was that?"

"Becquer. Said nothing the whole time. And according to you, he's got Montaldo's talent for always being on the winning side."

"You have a good memory, Finley."

"He's in on this, isn't he?"

"What's *this*?"

"Nearing . . .!"

"Okay. Hold your horses. I'll be right back."

He got up so quickly I thought he was heading for the door to get away from my questions for good. But what he had seen was a counter boy without a line. He came back with a teabag beginning to stain his cup of hot water. "Nothing about this on my allowance."

"Where am I, Nearing?"

"At the end of the line if you want to be. Hyde's right—there's no more danger for you."

"Every time you say Hyde or Vincent is right, I get the feeling I'm hearing half an answer."

"I don't owe *that* much to your father-in-law."

If he had been trying to take some air out of my sails, it worked. The only one who didn't want to talk about the Professor's past association with Roger Nearing more than Joe Carroll was Roger Nearing.

"But okay," he said, getting rid of his teabag. "Start with the Bureau. You're right—it's involved up to its hairline. But not just because they're clever and Machiavellian. Never underestimate inertia and confusion. They're vital to the functioning of the bureaucracy."

"How?"

"Different people with different ideas," he shrugged. "There are some who wanted to stop Paz simply because you don't kill foreign dignitaries on U.S. soil. Others wanted Paz stopped because assassination is a no-no *and* because they know Becquer from way back, trained with him, wanted to be standup guys for one of their almost-own. And then you have another group that won't go into mourning if things change in Bolivia and Montaldo is the first card in the deck to fall."

"How come they're the guys who came out on top?"

"Yup, that seems to be the question."

"What's the answer?"

"I'd say Becquer. He swung the fence-sitters when his intentions became clear. What's he get out of it? The usual things. Why be a bodyguard for Montaldo when there's something grander on the horizon? The reason he didn't open his mouth yesterday, by the way, is because Montaldo is on to him. For all practical purposes, Lerico's been head of security there lately. If there wasn't a gun in Becquer's ribs yesterday, there was something like it."

"So much for Lerico the unadorned thug."

He laughed; almost sincerely. "You don't forget anything, do you? Sure, he's a thug. He just liked the deal Montaldo offered him more than the alternative. It's called ambition."

"Yeah, I know all about ambition. If you're a gypsy cabbie, you want to have a dozen cars in your fleet. If you own a music store on a dead-end street, you want to open another one on Boston Common."

"I didn't say I admired their ambition."

"No, you haven't said a damn thing adding up to all those bodies."

His sigh said I had been entitled to one snap. "The decision was made to clear the ground for the real Paz."

"Just like that."

"You're not listening. The confusion factor has been there all along. Paz sets up Olmos. Someone at the Bureau hears from Bernstein . . ."

"Frank Vincent."

"It doesn't matter who."

"It matters."

"Stick to personalities, Finley, and you won't get anywhere. The big picture. The people come later."

"How could I have forgotten?"

"Someone from the Bureau passes on Bernstein's inquiry to the mission. Becquer has confirmation things are in motion. He doesn't expect anything to happen to him or Lerico because of Olmos, so that's why the address book is important. It's a map that's supposed to lead back to him and Lerico, push them on a plane out of here and away from responsibility. But Lerico smells a rat. How could he not after that thing in Queens?"

"That thing in Queens was a bloodbath."

"A bloodbath. By then Lerico's sure Becquer is playing with too many cards. So, he takes the wildest gamble his dim mind has ever taken and goes to Montaldo with his suspicions. He's in luck because Montaldo has already been worried about the media hush-hush."

"Where was the FBI during all this?"

I was afraid he would have backed off before another direct question, but he didn't. "This way and that. They knew what was going on, but if they could play everything by the numbers, they didn't have much incentive to jump off the fence. Olmos, the Mirandas, you in the parking lot—none of it created enough waves to end all their internal squabbling."

"So Stanton was killed because of fucking publicity!!??"

"Lack of it. That and the confusion in the Bureau hierarchy." He paused, finding some new wonder in his thoughts. "Think of it, Finley. Stanton was killed because the world's center of media information had no information and because the agency that likes to think of itself as the planet's strongest law enforcement body got comfortable with its inertia!"

Nothing at the tables around us made sense. A skel with a week's growth was reading the stock tables. A couple of teenagers were talking about nightclubs instead of being in school. A woman was wearing a running suit so she could eat some greasy chicken thing for breakfast.

"I'd imagine Paz and Becquer were getting pretty desperate at this point. That's why they went after you and Bernstein. Not even the Bureau could stay on the fence after that, they figured. Actually, I think they figured wrong because if Bernstein hadn't kicked up the fuss he did, the Bureau would still be wallowing in its inertia. But your cop friend made all that noise, so you ended up meeting Montaldo yesterday."

"Do you hear the whim in all this, Nearing?"

"I'm not deaf," he said, unperturbed.

What other answer had I expected? "And now? The Feds will protect Montaldo, but just so far?"

"There are always variables. A dedicated agent who takes directives more seriously than he's supposed to, that kind of thing."

"Something else to count on."

"Not too far."

"And what do you get out of telling me all this? And don't tell me it's the Professor. That was the first time, not today."

He put his nose down into his tea. I knew that whatever he came up with would be another half-truth, but even that suddenly seemed better than nothing. "The only thing worse than cowboys, Finley, are incompetent cowboys," he said. "The Hydes and Vincents are playing around in things they don't understand."

"But you do."

He didn't look like a securities executive anymore; his eyes were as cold as Lerico's. "I don't think the United States Government should be compromised by Young Republicans with badges," he said evenly. "It may seem to you we're just shuffling around corrupt politicos, but that isn't the case. Understandings have been reached. Agreements have been made. They require Montaldo to go on functioning on all cylinders."

"For now, you mean."

"Nothing lasts forever. But I'm talking policy, not philosophy. And some people have lost respect for the loop. They count on still being where they are long after their nominal superiors have retired to the Virginia hills. The arrogance of the Federal servant can be very destructive sometimes."

I thought of what Angela had said along the same lines; I didn't like the idea she had some of the same views as Nearing.

He pulled an agenda out of his pocket. It was written in Spanish and had numbers down one side. "Figure that Paz has five days maximum before the replacements for Becquer and Lerico arrive," he said. "The Bureau will drag its feet when it gets the applications for a security clearance, but it can't attract too much attention."

The paper turned out to be a detailed itinerary of Montaldo's public appearances for the next week. With everyone else accounted for, I figured it had come from either Montaldo himself or the flack.

"This might be helpful," Nearing said.

"For what?"

"For someone who doesn't want a killing on his watch."

I didn't like the idea of Bernstein's office being bugged, so I dismissed it. "Bernstein's a cop. With bosses."

"So you'll talk to him at my urging like you're probably talking with me at his."

"Why would he listen to me? And what do I care about Montaldo?"

"I can't imagine you care about him at all. You don't give a goddamn about the Bolivian ambassador to the UN, the president of Bolivia, probably not the president of the United States. But I have confidence in your self-righteousness, Finley. The self-righteousness that's scandalized to hear the real Banana Republic is right here with Hyde and Vincent."

"Don't leave yourself out."

He buttoned up his coat with a nod. "Sticks and stones. Be sure to look in your mailbox tomorrow. I thought I'd have a decent picture of Paz to give you, but we had a technical problem. The Bureau hasn't cornered the market on glitches."

"Don't count on that self-righteousness too far."

"What I'm counting on, Finley, is those children in Jackson Heights you never met and a would-be musician in Boston."

"You son of a bitch."

He stood with his plastic teacup. "Tell Joe we're even."

I watched him go over to the trash can at the door. The remains of his tea slopped out as he threw the cup inside. I knew how the tea felt.

* * *

Bernstein dropped by my apartment late that afternoon before going to work. The positive thing was that he had once again driven to the end of Brooklyn because he considered me so important. The negative thing was that he had that look of one part impatience and one part dread I had seen in the Rhode Island emergency room waiting for the doctor to get to his collarbone. What I told him about Nearing didn't relax him.

"This source of yours should change brands," he growled. "I'm going to keep an eye on this shithead Montaldo while Paz makes a run at him from one side and Hyde's running away from the other? How would I explain that at Police Plaza? He give you an idea about that, too?"

A woman across the courtyard was yelling at someone named Sharon for not cleaning up her room. It occurred to me I didn't know if Bernstein had a family, that all I really knew about him was that he had an apartment with a phone and a radio. I decided he was a widower, was secretly in love with McGill, but also intimidated by her and so tried to think he was secure in their professional relationship.

"I hear the speech, Finley, but I can't make out the words."

I hadn't been sure of them until they came out of my mouth, either. "We have a helluva lot of bodies over all this bullshit. Mr. and Mrs. Rabbit at the Vega may be the most wholesome people I've met lately."

"That and a MetroCard."

Sharon had heard enough and slammed a door, but the mother kept going. Mine always had, too. "I was told I'd be making this speech to you in my self-righteousness. I hate being predictable to scuzzballs."

"Go ahead. I won't tell anybody."

There was only one way to say it: "You can't drop it, Bernie."

He tried to look at ease about sitting back on my couch and raising one leg over another. The thought of getting himself untwisted again made me wince. "Like hell I can't. Check the hotels around the city recently? You got Russian, French, and Chinese sailors laid out all over the place with slugs in their head. It's the Big Apple. The entertainment goes on and on."

"But in the meantime, let's focus on the Bolivians. Paz is on third base. And both of us helped him get there."

The last of the afternoon light shone through the blinds directly into his hound dog face. He tried to stare through it. "How the hell did you last even 12 years in Mineola?"

"I didn't offend, and most of the time didn't even know what would have been offensive."

"You recommend it?"

"No."

"But?"

"No buts. Sometimes back in school, we'd be sitting around in the cafeteria and somebody would say, 'If you could be somebody else in life, who would it be?' You'd hear all the usual names—Willie Mays, Brando, one of the Kennedys. But I could never come up with a name. This one's glory, that one's money, fine, but not somebody else's whole life! I wanted to be me, Bernie. I still want to. And I mean this one here, not the one who did 12 years on Major Cases. It's what you got now that counts, right?"

He gave it a second, unwound himself without getting a hernia, and managed to get to his feet. "Give me that schedule." He pocketed Nearing's itinerary without giving it a glance. "We're not going anywhere without a picture of the real Victor Paz."

"Tomorrow, he said."

"*He* said! For all I know he's somebody who lives under your sofa. But I'll think about it. And keep in mind that even if it's doable, it's McGill and Masterson and nobody else. Straight moonlighting."

"I figured."

"Then figure this, too: Even if I decide to put an oar in, it'll be a harassment tactic, nothing else. Paz shows his face in the wrong place, you'll see me jumping up and down like an old woman who's had her purse snatched. Any Feds around will take it from there. Got it?"

"Why shouldn't I?"

"'Why shouldn't I?' Because I don't like that look on your face. You feel *right* about this."

"Sounds like a step up from being self-righteous."

He started to say something, then decided not to bother. As I walked him to the door, I wasn't all that sure of the difference, either.

SEVEN

I found the promised photo of Victor Paz in an unaddressed envelope in my mailbox the next morning. The picture showed a tall, thin man with a pencil mustache, swept back salt-and-pepper hair, and a black leather wristband handing money to a cashier in what appeared to be a cafe. He didn't look anything like Jaime Olmos, and the Campari advertisement next to the register could have been in La Paz, Singapore, or the Bronx.

I took the picture around to a Photostat place on Fourth Avenue, thinking of it as my ante in the pot. If Bernstein and the others could gamble their pensions, I could spring for a few buck's worth of copies. It took the kid behind the counter almost a half-hour to get the hang of the enlargement button and for me to be satisfied with the reproduction. To appease the gods of superstition I spread them around in my pockets before leaving the store to return home. When I called Bernstein, the radio was playing in the background again, on an all-news station; I wondered if it was ever off and if it was irritating neighbors in Turtle Bay, Greenwich Village, or Inwood. We arranged to meet at one o'clock in a Madison Avenue coffee shop a couple of blocks away from the Bolivian mission. I thought it optimistic of me to fill in the time by setting up appointments with two prospective clients. What was pessimistic was to slip one of the Paz photocopies into the *Columbia Encyclopedia* the Professor had given me, on an **N** page headed by an entry for Field Marshal Ney. I couldn't see Paz looking there after he had murdered me and started ripping apart the apartment.

It was in that merry frame of mind that I drove over to the city. The coffee shop was one of those museums of tire-sized Danishes on the counter, a Greek and his wife going at it over the register, and wall booths designed for midgets. With his sling, Bernstein looked like he had been squeezed into his booth weeks ago and had given up hope of ever getting out again. On the other hand, he seemed to go out of his way to cram into tight spots. What kind of a character flaw was that?

"Good news and bad news," he said, after glancing at the Paz photos and setting them aside.

"Always start with the bad."

"Panama City ricocheted on us. My captain thought he was being a sport by not taking the transmission charges out of my salary."

"He knows more than that."

"Everybody knows everything, Finley. That's not what this is about. What my captain knows, in particular, is that he doesn't want to hear another word about Victor Paz or Jaime Olmos."

"The good news?"

"Masterson has rotten teeth."

"What?"

He smiled quizzically. "Yesterday afternoon he took a walk across the street from the embassy and wrote down the names of all the dentists with offices facing the building. Then he called up the guy who's been gouging him for bridges just in case one of the names rang a bell. One did. The gouger sent him over to see Harold Rothberg, D.D.S., this morning."

"So?"

"So Harold Rothberg is going to stick all his high-class pa-tients into six or seven chairs for the next few days. The eighth room is for us."

I didn't know why that was good news: Masterson's inspira-tion added up to too much of a practical commitment by all con-cerned. Bernstein loved seeing my expression, too. "Is this the right part or the self-righteous part?"

"Okay, okay. You look at that schedule?"

"Yeah. Can we count on getting last-minute changes?"

"Why not? My mailbox seems to be in the public domain."

"Okay. Then here's what we got so far. McGill says there's one car with two Feds parked directly across from the mission. When Montaldo went down to the UN this morning, he had nobody with him but his driver and that irritating little p.r. man. In about ten blocks, McGill says, about half a dozen cars got in between Montaldo and the Feds. Not bad for surveillance, but crap for security."

"At the UN?"

"The Barnum and Bailey circus could have gotten to Montaldo and used him as a trampoline. The Feds stayed in their car on First Avenue."

The short order cook had Paz's kind of salt-and-pepper hair. I had a feeling I was going to be noticing people like him too much for a few days.

"Assuming you have some spare time, I worked out a little schedule for Rothberg's office."

It was the kind of duty sheet that had taken me hours to wrestle into sense in Mineola; he had even used an NYPD form. But there was nothing complicated about it: It carried only four names and provided for extended stretches when nobody had any duty at all. "If he wants to sneak out at night, that's his lookout. I took your source's schedule very literally. If it said he was going home after lunch, that's where I assume he's going. I also happen to have a few hundred other things on my desk."

Most of the schedule was meetings within the United Nations. There were also two nights of dinners at midtown hotels, two official lunches at midtown restaurants, the opening of a new Bolivian airline office on Fifth Avenue, and a City Hall meeting with a deputy mayor. But all those dates blurred when I read the itinerary for the following Monday.

"Glad you agree," Bernstein said, seeing my reaction.

It was made to order for Paz. First, Montaldo was going to Jackson Heights to meet with what were described as "community leaders." From there he would go across the Whitestone Bridge to the Bronx Zoo. "What the hell is an Andean bear?"

Bernstein took out his notebook and opened it with a flourish. "The Andean bear is the only survivor of so-called short-faced

mammals that roamed across the Americas during the Pleisto-
cene epoch two million years ago," he read from a Xeroxed page
clipped to the notebook. "Also known as the spectacled bear, the
cow-eating bear, the red-fronted bear, and—listen to this—the
black puma. A puma's a lion. What the hell does that have to do
with a bear?" He snapped the book closed again. "Anyway, he's
making a little speech when they deliver one of these things to
the zoo."

"It's perfect."

The fat man nodded. "Out in the open for three or four hours.
Maybe I should zero in on Monday and forget the rest of it."

"It'd save you some stories for your captain."

"It might. And I sure don't want to ask you to take most of the
shifts in Doctor Rothberg's office."

"No, you don't."

"On the other hand, suppose Paz doesn't see the same possibilities for Monday as we do? We can't risk being presumptuous."

"Christ, no."

"Okay, then. Your first turn is . . ." He made a show of consult-
ing the sheet in my hand. "How about that! In 15 minutes!"

"What a coincidence!"

"Keep one thing in mind, Finley. We're on a sighting mission
here, nothing else. No bullshit."

"Don't worry. I don't have your health plan."

"Good thought," he said, motioning to the waitress for the
check. "And remember I want to keep mine."

* * *

Bernstein hadn't been exaggerating about Rothberg's office. The dentist had more adjustable black chairs than a bar-
ber school—each in a room with its own cabinets, torture tools,
and piped in Mozart. The chairs were outnumbered only by the
nurses and technicians who scurried in and out of the studios
along both sides of an L-shaped corridor. There must have been
down times at Grand Central Station with fewer people running
around. Our stakeout spot was a storeroom for cartons of dental
supplies. With its street window, it seemed like a waste of costly
Upper East Side real estate, but I decided to keep my opinion to

myself until Rothberg asked my advice on how to get better use from his facilities.

McGill gave me five minutes to take in her instructions on how to use a two-way radio model I'd never seen before and to memorize the code words for when Montaldo was leaving the mission, when Paz was spotted, when the Feds disappeared altogether, and when other whens arose. I guess I wasted two of the minutes taking in the fact that the box for the radio was sitting on one of Rothberg's crates. Whatever Bernstein had to say about his pension, he had obviously sprung for radios that hadn't come out of the NYPD storeroom. It seemed like the best argument I'd heard yet for using a cell phone, but neither McGill nor Masterson was apparently up to defying the fat man's ban on anything invented after 1980. Either that or they didn't think I was up to memorizing three new numbers.

She was also annoyed to hear that I hadn't bulldozed other cars out of the way to park directly in front of Rothberg's and that I would have to go back over to Lexington to retrieve my car and move it to the garage on the block where she had negotiated special privileges for us. In the interests of being equally thorny, I wondered why she had chosen the garage on the north side of the street instead of the one facing it on the south side. Her solemn reply was that the north side garage's john was all the way in the back, while the south side garage had a toilet next to the entrance space where it would be ideal for keeping a tail car; since even FBI agents had to go sometimes, she lectured, she was betting they would get used to going to the south side garage and she didn't want them noticing our cars. As I hurried over to Lexington, I had two thoughts: that everyone else had been putting a lot of cash and reflection into my spasms for keeping an eye on Montaldo and that I had been out of Major Cases for a century and a half.

The Feds were parked a couple of doors down from Fifth, across the street from the mission on Rothberg's side. During my first four-hour shift neither of them moved to take a leak in the south side garage or to do anything else. Although my view from the stock room took in only the driver (a muscular blond entranced by every word of the New York *Post*), the quiet street made it likely that I would hear his partner do something uproarious like getting out to stretch his legs.

There wasn't much traffic in and out of the mission itself; certainly, no one with salt-and-pepper hair or as tall and thin as Paz. Of course, that said nothing. Anyone devious enough to set up Jaime Olmos wasn't going to blanch before hair dye or hesitate about dieting on chocolate layer cakes. Then, too, the Jackson Heights witnesses had said *two* Con Edison workers had visited the Miranda house and there had also been two guys in the Toyota that had come at us in Rhode Island. The second man could have been anyone at all entering the townhouse on the pretext of wanting to know more about Andean bears.

We underestimated Montaldo's self-preservation instincts. The very first day, when he had been scheduled to attend a reception at the Regency Hotel, he never left the premises. It was the same story the next day when he ought to have attended a reception at the Drake. Over the first three days, in fact, my only outing was to follow him and the Feds down to City Hall for the meeting with the deputy mayor. The highlight of that trip was spotting Bernstein and McGill wolfing down hot dogs in City Hall Park. Evidently, the fat man wasn't as convinced as he had sounded that Paz would make his try during the excursion to the Bronx Zoo.

That was his opinion. As I let myself into Rothberg's office Sunday evening, I didn't have the slightest doubt I was wasting my time, that going after Montaldo to a First Avenue dinner with other Latin American diplomats would only get me another expenditure of gas I would never be compensated for. Because Bernstein had drawn the last shift Saturday night, the stock room reeked of the cigars he had been content to extinguish on a saucer. I started to open the window for some air and found a reason to be thankful I was a middle-aged machine beginning to rust. A few years before, I wouldn't have had so much trouble with the latch and would yank the window open so fast I would have alarmed the guy tying his shoe next to the parked car in front of Rothberg's. I had never seen him before, but what I could see was that he wasn't doing much of a job with his laces. How could he be when his hands kept traveling over a perfectly made bow while he glanced up toward Fifth, toward the Feds in their blue Ciera?

Since I didn't dare tickle the guy's peripheral vision by widening the blinds, I had to make do with what I made out between the slats. He was much younger than Paz, probably not yet thirty, with curly black hair and a bladelike nose. He wore a heavy, off-white three-quarter jacket that had probably cost him the equivalent of any five items in my closet. It wasn't hard imagining him operating a light that could blind a driver.

Then he was up, giving his left foot an elaborate and phony testing turn in the air and proceeding toward the park. As he went out of view, the agent behind the wheel of the Ciera turned a newspaper page.

The standing orders were that I contact Bernstein at the slightest sign of something suspicious. Had I seen something suspicious? Maybe. Curly might have also just been scouting the terrain for boosting a car or might have lived on the block and developed his own suspicions about the Feds always sitting in their Ciera. In Bernstein's place, would I have wanted to be pulled off the couch from some *60 Minutes* interview with another fired whistleblower to listen to a suspicion as slight as mine? Of course not.

So, I called at home anyway on Rothberg's hall phone. He outsmarted me: He wasn't home and didn't have a machine. So much for the greatest tactical planning since Hannibal had crossed the Alps.

Then Montaldo's limo drove up in front of the townhouse and, no more than five seconds later, Montaldo himself emerged, apparently from behind a foyer curtain with the running plan of a sprinter. I didn't have much choice: I used McGill's squawk box to tell her or Masterson, whoever was on the other end, that we had a Turkey Situation. By her code, that wasn't as grave as a Goose Situation and hardly meant a Rabbit Situation, but it was more serious than the everyday Chicken Situation. As I left the storeroom to get my car, I decided McGill did have a sense of humor, after all: The turkey wasn't the target who just *might* have been in jeopardy, it was me.

The limo was pulling away from the mission as I reached the street. The two linemen in the Bureau car had also made progress: They had turned on their headlights. The Sunday man in the garage booth stood up as if ready to cross-examine me on my time card, but sat down again when he saw the car I went for. I was back out on the street in time to see the Ciera pass. I counted three cars between Montaldo and the Feds. The linemen were clearly not the agents Nearing had in mind when he had talked about some conscientious G-Man fouling up Hyde's scenario.

I used the red light at Park to get past the linemen and get within two cars of the limo. When the light changed, I startled the young Asian couple in the Audi next to me by cutting out in front of them. Only as I was getting back into line did it occur to me the Feds might think I was Paz. Moral: If you do something half-assed, go all the way because you can't erase the first mistake. That made it only logical for me to cut off the last car behind Montaldo at Third. It seemed better for my mental health not to check the mirror to see if the linemen had also been coming up.

The limo double-parked before a fancy Spanish restaurant with tan curtains on all the windows. With the traffic rumbling down First Avenue at an Indy 500 pace, I dove for the bus stop several doors down. The few yards from the limo to the restaurant door were enough for a dozen Victor Paz snipers to get at Montaldo, but he crossed the sidewalk safely in a few quick strides. As soon as he disappeared inside, I went back to exhaling. My hands had become so sweaty they didn't want to unstick themselves from the wheel. Had there ever been a more asinine surveillance in the history of police work?

The radio on the seat next to me kicked in—loudly enough for two kids waiting at the bus shelter with their mother to look curious about the crackling noise. It was Masterson saying he was on his way to "look over Turkey." I smiled at the kids—obviously like a loon because they both backed up as though I had just fled Bellevue. I was about to tell Masterson not to bother coming when a car caught by the light pulled up next to me. It was a green Ciera, and I wondered how the Feds had managed to repaint the body in just a few blocks. But it wasn't the linemen, it was a weathered gentleman with the face of a dachshund and a high crest of white hair. Sitting next to him was Curly.

Had we advanced to a Goose Situation? The red light didn't give me much time to decide. If I called in a Goose to Masterson, he would follow Bernstein's orders and rattle the cages of the linemen, who were now coasting into a space on the west end of the avenue a half-block behind me. I was the one who should have run back to the blue Ciera screaming that Paz was in the restaurant and that Dachshund and Curly were keeping their motor going for his getaway.

Montaldo died over and over again while I made up my mind. Then Dachshund's cigarette called it: He was so casual about fingering one of his Marlboros out of the box above the steering wheel that I couldn't accept he was waiting for anything but the light to change. When Curly leaned over to snatch another cigarette from the box, I was sure they had already done what they had set out to do: monitor the proximity of the Feds to the limo.

I was still congratulating myself for not blowing everything with the Feds with a false alarm when the light changed and Dachshund hit the gas. I went after him; with Montaldo safe in the restaurant, there was no reason not to. In fact, the only thing better than nabbing Paz in the act, I rehearsed my speech to Bernstein, was getting him the night before—quietly, no fuss, medals handed around to all of us while Hyde and Vincent seethed. All I had to do was follow the two mopes back to Paz.

Reality returned in Germantown when Dachshund ran a light to swing west on 86th Street. Had he seen me? I didn't want to believe it, so I didn't. I told myself he was just going through the numbers, seeing if anyone tried to squeeze the light as he had. I had little choice but to wait for the clicks and let a bus trundle over the intersection ahead of me. By the time I got up to Third Avenue, there was no more green Ciera.

I didn't want it to matter. I'd already made an appointment with Victor Paz for Monday, for somewhere between a church hall in Jackson Heights and the bear cages of the Bronx Zoo. I didn't know the exact spot or time yet, but that was okay, too. As Angela might have reminded me, an invisible place was supposed to stay invisible until you reached it.

* * *

Masterson stayed with me until after Montaldo was back at the mission. He was annoyed I hadn't reported Dachshund and Curly as a Rabbit Situation, but once he got that out of his system, he proposed a drink before I slogged back to Brooklyn. At one of those Second Avenue Irish places with the beer reeking from the wood of the bar he told me he was going to bed down at the precinct instead of commuting back and forth to Riverdale. I knew as soon as he said it that I wasn't going home, either.

With the help of a couple of Johnny Walkers I found out Masterson had been working with Bernstein for seven years, he was mildly resentful of Bernstein's preference for McGill, and there weren't two better cops on the planet than Bernstein and McGill. I also heard how Mrs. Bernstein had walked out on Bernstein for an EMS doctor six years ago, how Bernstein had moved into a Chelsea walkup with two cats, how McGill had an on-and-off boyfriend who worked at the Met Museum, how McGill had been waiting forever for him to be more on than off, and how Bernstein and McGill belonged to the nineteenth century for the way they both pretended not to be interested in one another. "She may have a cell phone and know how to work a computer, but she's as old-fashioned as he is," Masterson said, bewilderment in his voice. "We don't even joke about it anymore in the squad room. I don't know—they seem to want an awful lot from each other before they even consider the next step. Know what I'm saying?"

I did and envied both.

"I'd invite you to sack out at the precinct," Masterson said when he grabbed his coat to go, "but that might raise too many questions."

"I'm okay. I'll see you tomorrow."

"Odds are nothing goes down, you know."

"It'll go down."

"Because you want it to?"

"Because it'll go down."

He had no answer to that and strolled out of the bar with a lazy wave. I had another scotch for the road, then drove west to

leave my car in an Eighth Avenue lot for the night. Then I headed
for the Hotel Vega.

It hadn't been the Vega specifically until Masterson had gone
into his snit about the Rabbit Situation with Dachshund and
Curly. That had reminded me of Mr. and Mrs. Rabbit. Masterson
had also started my engine on another point: Granted that Paz
and Becquer had sent Olmos to the Vega as a setup, but why
the Vega in particular? Why not the flophouse down the street
or the one over on the next block? Had the Vega been chosen at
random? Had Becquer just passed it one day on his way to some
official function? The random didn't appeal to me as an explanation for anything.

I had a high school reunion feeling walking into the tomb of a
lobby: Now that I'd confirmed everybody was still in worse shape
than I was, what the hell was I doing there? I focused on the
changes. The old toothless guy who had been sleeping on his right
palm last time had switched to his left palm. A fat woman who had
been wearing stockings up to her knees last time had gotten some
new rubber bands. The black-and-white TV was off. And most
obviously, Mr. and Mrs. Rabbit were nowhere to be seen.

Manning the desk was a scrawny kid who might or might not
have come out of the hutch, but who had certainly come out of a
few detox centers. Like all respectable hoteliers he was worried I
didn't have luggage; like all Vega desk personnel, he scanned me
for signs of the cash he would find on the body if I turned out to
be a jumper. His compromise verdict was that I was entitled to a
second-floor room for sixty dollars. When I bid forty, he glanced
over at the closed office door, then nodded that, yes, that would
be enough of a rip-off of the Rabbits. I took my key, he made a
mandatory move toward the till drawer with my four tens, then I
whirled back just in time to see one ten going into the drawer and
the other three into his pants pocket. The resignation that descended over his face made him look ripe for earning another ten.

"It belongs to the hotel," he said, clutching at the register.
"What's so important you want to see?"

I didn't have to make up a story; realizing his voice had probably carried over to the office door, he spun the register back

at me and grabbed the ten in my hand. "Thirty seconds or two pages, whichever comes first."

I went back to the date Jaime Olmos had been killed. The name Victor Paz had been written like a chicken scratch; I suppose I had expected to see something a little sturdier from a seaman. There hadn't been more than a dozen new names a week, and with one exception none of them qualified as finalists in a penmanship contest. The exception was ROSE MCTAGGART, whose neat loops said parochial school nun.

"That's enough."

I slapped the punk's hand away. Bernstein had said the fire escape made it unnecessary for the killer to pass the front desk. But how could the killer have known about the fire escape unless he had doped it out earlier?

"You're back to last year."

He was right: I'd already gone back through people who had spent Christmas at the Vega and I was closing in on Thanksgiving. The register hadn't told me anything.

"Still want the room?"

I took the insolent question upstairs with me to the second floor. My instincts had been impeccably professional in looking at the register, I told myself; who was to say ROSE MCTAGGART hadn't been the shooter?

My room seemed smaller than Olmos's but was the same heap of a bed, mismatched night tables, decrepit bureau, and scuzzy sink. A few flies had died on the ceiling during the Ed Koch administration, but I couldn't make out any other wildlife. I was open to the argument that was because of my eyesight, not because the animal kingdom wasn't teeming somewhere.

I pulled together three wire hangers and hung my coat and jacket over them on the wall bar that served as a closet, then got my cigarettes, notepad, and pen from the pockets. By the time I'd thrown two saggy pillows up against the headboard and sprawled out, I knew the notepad and pen were superfluous. Like the headless chicken running around the barnyard, though, I still had my routines. I lighted a cigarette, poised my pen over the notepad, and tried to think of something relevant to the Vega that had eluded me. What I ended up doing was going through the cigarette trying to put a face on the man (that much I could tell) muttering in the room behind my sink. I was down to the filter before realizing the voice belonged to a radio, to one of those droning imbeciles who demanded the right to bear an Uzi against the IRS. The people who called up to argue with clowns like that, I thought, were worse than the halfwits who phoned in to say Uzis weren't nearly enough, what about Howitzers? The people who called up to argue good sense were the opposite of Phil Ortega: They helped keep everything on the air so they *were* Phil Ortega.

I used the pen to write down good things. The Professor had been worried enough about me to risk exposing some old secret that shamed him. Rosemary Stanton had scraped off her door to enjoy at least a few hours of confidence that she could go on alone. Whenever she let her eyes drift off beyond the Rio de la Plata and thought of New York cops, Angela would think about me instead of that fabled patrolman who had dragged the dead horse from Kosciusko Street to Orange Street because he couldn't spell Kosciusko in his report

Why were the bad things the same as the good things?

Because they were all visible. I had come to the Vega instead of somewhere else because I had been to the Vega before. Jaime Olmos had been killed in the Vega instead of somewhere else because that was where Bernstein, McGill, and Masterson had told me he had been killed. There had never been anything random or even mysterious about my starting points.

I lighted another cigarette and took it out into the hall, to the window with the fire escape. The pull ladder dropped to an alley that had a low fence blocking off the adjoining street. It reminded me of the alley behind the High Note. I thought of the cello music that Rosemary had needed to put herself to sleep and I could picture Jaime Olmos hearing the same flawed sounds. If I wanted to shoot somebody up on the third floor, I realized, I only had to negotiate the low street fence, be quiet about the pull ladder, and get upstairs. Mr. and Mrs. Rabbit wouldn't have seen me tonight, either.

The alley and the fire escape were an invisible place.

Where I had started.

EIGHT

Rothberg's office was already in full swing when I showed up at 7:30 Monday morning. Patients had been stowed in three chairs, a drill was humming, and the receptionist was assuring a giraffe of a woman that the doctor would have her in and out in plenty of time for her own office. Bernstein was in the storeroom with Jack Fine, the Connecticut cop who had driven us from Mystic to Port Chester. I tried to look casual about such unorthodox reinforcements and went over to the window to check on the mission. Frank Vincent was just coming out of the building. Bernstein and Fine stuck their noses through the slats I held open. "Hyde's with him," Bernstein said. "Their car's around on Fifth."

I was about to ask about the linemen, whom I hadn't noticed on the way in when Bernstein's radio barked out with McGill's voice. Once again I had underestimated their preparations because she had been busy checking out Montaldo's limousine with a bomb squad friend at its 73rd Street garage. What she was reporting now was that she was following the chauffeur down to the mission.

"This guy's already shown us he's pretty versatile," Bernstein said to my surprise. "Guns, bombs, glare lights. That limo blows up in the tunnel or on the bridge, we got more problems than who'll be the new Bolivian ambassador. Okay, Jack, get going. Stay in front as long as you can. If he wants to pass you, let him. But try to stay on his tail then."

Fine gathered up a city map he had been studying and slipped out. Bernstein began to reach for a cigar, then decided needling me would be just as good. "You shave in front of a store window?"

"The Vega. And their showers actually work."

He thought it over before saying: "This isn't a coin story, Finley. If we're lucky, it won't be any kind of story."

"Sure. And Fine has nothing better to do on his day off."

"He thinks he owes me."

I could have done without that answer. Whatever Fine thought he owed Bernstein with a late-night drive through Connecticut and now a long trip through Manhattan and Queens up to the Bronx seemed to be as much of a national debt as Roger Nearing's to the Professor.

The limo arrived in front of the townhouse, and I started for the door. "No hurry," Bernstein said, grabbing my arm. "Fine's in front and McGill behind. We'll give them a couple of blocks."

He swung his sling back to the blinds and pressed down on a slat. "You're getting more mobility."

"Yeah, the Mets want me to pitch Opening Day. But there's a good side. Every time it jabs I remember what I owe these fuckers."

"Maybe I should have broken a collarbone."

"No, what you have to do, Finley, is get back to the gray world with the rest of us. Black holes are for scientists, and even they're smart enough to stay billions of miles away from them. Here they come."

The flack stood in front of the door in a neat gray coat with a black fur collar; he was tugging on leather gloves. Montaldo was behind him, his foot still in the street door, imparting some last instructions to somebody out of sight in the foyer.

"Where do you think that schedule came from?" Bernstein asked. "That little guy there?"

"Or Montaldo himself. When you get right down to it, he's the only one you can really trust to worry about his security."

Bernstein thought that plausible. Montaldo came out to the stoop. His coat was a twin of the flack's; he also wore a jaunty brown fedora with a tiny purple feather. The chauffeur held the door open until both his passengers were in the back. He slammed the door and went around to the wheel without leaning in and shooting them. I considered that a good start.

We got out to the lobby of Rothberg's building just as the chauffeur and Montaldo finished conferring about something over the front seat. The limo started east, and I counted to eight before Vincent rolled by in a black Caprice. Hyde was sitting next to him and talking on a cell phone. Then McGill went by in a brown Corolla.

"He's made other changes and I don't like that little palaver with the driver," Bernstein said as we hurried down to the garage. "So just in case he's decided to switch from the bridge to the tunnel, you head directly for the tunnel. We'll join up out at the church."

"So I get stuck with the toll? No, thanks. I'll take the bridge."

He didn't have time to argue, but he muttered a lot as he got into his car and rolled out for at least the moral victory of being first back on the street. I stayed with him over to Second Avenue, where he suddenly swerved out ahead of a panel truck and shot downtown for the tunnel. I ended up with less than even his moral victory when I committed to the bridge's upper ramp. Too late I saw the chauffeur maneuver over into the lower ramp—probably what Montaldo had been telling him to do before they had set off. I had just enough time to spot Vincent and McGill inching along after the limo before I was rumbling out over the upper ramp grating. Riding over the river to Long Island City, I had too many visions of the explosion scenario Bernstein had tossed off ever so casually.

Once in Queens, I made straight down Roosevelt Avenue for the church in Jackson Heights. It was a tour of Finley's Greatest Hits, with the appropriate soundtrack headache coming from the #7 El overhead. Off to your right, Ladies and Gentlemen, a chiropractor named Schmidt who didn't worry about slipped discs as much as the checks he cashed from patients desperate to avoid surgery. Off to your left, the pharmacy presently owned by Patrick Hardy but probably soon to be under new management while Patrick paid for his donkey sins. And up ahead, of course, the remains of Hector Miranda's car service.

The church was on a serene street of two-family homes up a few blocks from all the clattering along Roosevelt. It was a typical Catholic graystone of the 1950s with a broad sidewalk plaza, built for Mahoneys and O'Connells but now maintained by Martinezes and Perezes. The announcement board outside said that I had missed Sunday's sermon on the PASION Y MUERTE DE CRISTO.

There were a couple of dozen spiffily dressed men and women standing in front of the church; they looked like wedding guests waiting for the bride to arrive. I slid into a space that gave me a direct line on the church's basement office that was supposed to be the center of the action. I saw Masterson a couple of cars down and weighed the idea of using the walkie-talkie to suggest one of us take a better look at the far side of the church, but dismissed it. Bernstein had been emphatic about using the radio only as a last resort; in case something went wrong he didn't want someone popping up to tell *Eyewitness News* about this cryptic communication between cops on the scene minutes before the disaster.

Jack Fine came along in a gray Cougar. I gave Bernstein another point for Fine's New York plates. Maybe it was the wedding look of the gang in front of the church, but I gazed into my crystal ball and saw McGill and Bernstein eventually getting married. I hoped I got an invitation.

That sentimental moment almost cost me. Instead of the limo coming along next, it was the black Caprice with Vincent and Hyde. I squirmed to get lower in my seat even as I told myself it was too late, that I had been spotted. But the Feds had other priorities than what felt like my tenth mistake on the morning. Unlike Fine, who had continued down the block, Vincent stopped directly in front of the church; a second later he and Hyde were barging through the crowd toward the basement entrance like cops chasing a pickpocket in Times Square on New Year's Eve. There weren't *that* many people, and it was a soccer field of a sidewalk, but one or the other of them seemed to bump every Bolivian in sight. By the time Vincent and Hyde reached the entrance, the guests had more in common than wanting to shake Ambassador Montaldo's hand: They would all remember such boorish FBI agents.

And I knew that had been the point.

My old friend the ferret showed up in the general vicinity of my bowels. It was late in the day to realize it, but Victor Paz wasn't just a Roger Nearing photo, wasn't just the It in a game of Police Tag, and wasn't just food for meditation in the sleazy hotel of your choice. At that very moment, it dawned on me, Paz was getting into a Ciera with Dachshund and Curly for a trip to the Bronx Zoo. At that very moment, as well, someone—McGill or Bernstein or Fine or me—might have entered the last hour of his life as surely as Montaldo. Because sure as hell what was happening in the church basement was Vincent and Hyde doing one last riff for establishing their good intentions before witnesses.

My eyes dulled over as the two of them came back up from the basement. Hyde said something that looked apologetic to some of the waiting people. Vincent marched out into the gutter to wave ostentatiously up the block. A moment later the limo came into view. A bull of a man with more hair on his lip than head nodded to Hyde's explanation and passed it on to an equally hefty woman dressed in pink. Nods spread all over the plaza. How could anyone begrudge a scuff mark on a shoe or a nudge in the ribs if it helped guarantee Ambassador Montaldo's safety?

There was applause from the crowd when Montaldo stepped out of the limo, and I knew I was wasting my time at the church. I pulled away from the curb and rolled down to Masterson. He looked confused to see me breaking cover. "Tell Bernstein I'm going to the zoo."

"That's not the plan."

"Screw the plan."

I meditated on bears on the way over the Whitestone Bridge. I gave deep thought to Andean bears and polo bears and grizzlies. If the thing Montaldo was presenting to the zoo was called a spectacled bear, it figured to have markings around the eyes that resembled glasses. Which made me think of Paz and how he might have changed his appearance since Nearing's photo. Glasses? Why not? Shaved his head? Why not? Why not anything at all? I'd even have to take a close look at the guy cleaning out the shit and banana peels in the orangutan cages.

* * *

What I had to do before anything was wait. I made such great time I arrived twenty minutes before the zoo opened. There were six or seven clusters of people in front of the entrance turnstiles. I parked across the street from a firehouse a couple of blocks away, then walked back and bought a coffee from a lunch wagon. Finally, a guard pushed back the gates in front of the turnstiles. I almost spat out my coffee when I saw that the woman tousling the hair of an excited four-year-old going through the turnstile ahead of her was McGill. I hadn't been the only one to ditch Bernstein's plan.

A few bucks later I was out of the Bronx and inside the International Wildlife Park, as the signs declared. The .38 in the back of my belt didn't feel all that adequate to dealing with charging tigers and rhinos, but it was what I had. I hurried up the narrower of the two paths a few yards past the turnstiles. I hadn't seen where McGill had gone, and the smaller path promised a rise for getting a good view of who was where.

I was wrong. The damn path kept winding further and further away from the lower lane and toward a fenced-off highway that looked like Pelham Park. Ten minutes of this and I was back in Disney's Lost Forest. In the middle of the zoo, I was lost! Even the signs pointing to the Bengali Express and the Baboon Highlands seemed to have been staked into the ground by explorers who had then scampered back to civilization.

And then a small girl squealed from around a bend ahead of me, her mother laughed, and I felt brave again.

I ended up on a Japanese garden-type bridge. I recognized the flamingoes fluttering their feathers along a bank below me, but wasn't too good on the other birds. A sign pointed me toward the bear pits.

Then I saw Curly.

He was walking along a path perpendicular to the bridge, toting a toolbox and dressed like a maintenance worker. He looked capable of belting out "Whistlin' While I Work" for the school group passing him. A chubby kid swiped another kid's Red Sox cap and was so intent on ducking a punch in retaliation that he bumped into the toolbox.

I cringed.

Nothing happened.

Curly yanked away the box, the chubby kid looked embarrassed, and Curly kept going. I made sure there was a thick branch between us before I took out my radio. It was too soon for Montaldo to have arrived, but I had to warn McGill. I gave her what amounted to a Goose Situation and the location, then put the radio back in my pocket.

Curly continued his casual but purposeful walk past the quarry of polar bears; the animals looked like they had been sprayed with orange paint. The idea of a bomb on the bridge or in the tunnel had been nerves; the idea of a bomb in the toolbox was too strong even for my ferret. Not that it didn't try. But how could I be impressed when the whole goddamn zoo suddenly felt like it was gnawing at me?

In one of the cage plazas, genuine maintenance people were busy laying a microphone wire from the back of a wooden platform to a lectern. A finicky man in a brown suit, apparently immune to the cold, was barking a slew of orders, but none of the workmen seemed to pay any attention to him. Curly paused for a look at the preparations, then went on to the iron railing behind the platform. Even fifty yards behind him I made out the shaggy brown beast with golden patches on the forehead and snout. It might have been a brown bear that had been scorched in a fire, but then I read the sign for the ceremonies that left no doubt I was seeing an ANDEAN OR SPECTACLED BEAR (TREMARCTOS ORNATUS).

Curly leaned off the rail, glanced at the workmen again, and went on past the platform. The finicky man in the brown suit saw him, and I had a bad feeling was about to challenge Curly's credentials. But then he went back to his supervising.

Why didn't I take out Curly then and there? Because of the toolbox and because of Victor Paz. I didn't know what was in the box, not for sure, and didn't consider it much of a gain if Curly saw me coming and got to use whatever was in it against the maintenance people instead of Montaldo. I also smelled Paz nearby with every step of Curly's reconnaissance. By now I thought I knew something about the bastard: Victor Paz was an actor. The stage had to be set completely for his entrance. He must have loved the idea of the platform for the speech making. Montaldo might have thought the platform and lectern were for him, but Victor Paz had

been aiming all along for a last-minute replacement of the star for
the opening curtain.

Curly kept going past the eagles and cultures toward the parking lot. I was about to fall back to radio McGill when I saw Jack
Fine sauntering toward me. He passed Curly without a second
look, then snagged his step at seeing me. I shook my head, but
he came right for me anyway.

"Bernie says . . ."

"Fuck Bernie. Right behind you."

Fine saw enough in my face not to spin around and yell GAD-
ZOOKS, but not much more than that. "That was him?"

"No, but he's going for him. Where's Bernstein?"

"They'll be here in five minutes. He wants you and me gone,
said to go back to his place and wait for him."

"Then do it, Jack."

I didn't wait for more. When I got to the edge of the parking lot,
Curly was opening the back of a red utility truck with the lettering
ATLANTIC WIRING. It was one of only a couple of dozen vehicles,
and most of the others were bunched against a fence for employees. Fine's gray Cougar sat only a lane away from the truck.

Dachshund came out of the truck cab and walked around to
the back to talk to Curly; he too wore a maintenance uniform.
They did a lot of nodding. If ATLANTIC WIRING had been the
truck at the Miranda house, it shouldn't have been hard to find
traces of Con Edison blue beneath its red repainting. The toolbox,
on the other hand, had been a false alarm; Curly simply dumped
it in the back, its use as a prop ended.

I had to step back behind a tree as Dachshund suddenly
gazed around more vigilantly and Curly unpocketed a cell phone
and rapidly punched out a number. I didn't think they were calling the Weather.

"Paz?" Fine, at my elbow again, asked.

"Bet on it."

"McGill's here somewhere."

"Great. But they're here and Paz is somewhere else."

He looked offended. "What're you saying, Finley?"

"I say you keep watch on these two until they move from here. I'd guess one is a backup for Paz and the other is for the getaway. As soon as the backup leaves, radio me and McGill and then you take the driver." He began to object. "Citizen's arrest, for Christ sake! You're a cop down here on a day off to see the animals. Instead, you see this guy in the parking lot near your car acting suspiciously."

I had enlarged the Fuck Finley Club by another member. "What I was about to ask, hot shot, is what you'll be up to in the meantime."

"I know Paz better than anyone," I lied. "See you later."

When I got back to the bear cages, McGill was already there, trying to look interested in the orange polar bears. She had added a black woolen cap to her bomber jacket. The workmen had just about completed the platforming and the mike wiring. McGill saw me, looked right through me, then went back to the bears. That struck me as a step backward after our solid communing in Bernstein's office.

I ambled around the plaza near the bear pits, counting four separate paths into the platform area. Add the strip behind the platform for viewing the bears that led away east and west and there were six possible entry points. That was five too many. I sat down on a bench for a cigarette. There were maybe half a dozen people making the rounds of the animals. The adults—an old-timer in a stained green raincoat and the grandmother of a girl who looked too much like Little Lulu—seemed more entertained than the kids by the coatimundis and other packrat creatures. An ice cream wagon attached to a bicycle went by. I looked over the guy pedaling. What was more suspicious than somebody selling ice cream on a winter Monday morning? But whatever disguise Victor Paz had chosen, I knew, it was unlikely to include acne.

* * *

The ruckus started from two directions at once. First, there was the school group I'd seen back at the Japanese bridge, now overrunning the bear pit path behind McGill. From the way the brawny coach in charge ordered the kids to form a circle around him, I gathered his bear lecture had been billed as a highlight of the excursion. I would have also bet that football coach, science teacher, or whatever he was, had some nickname related to bears, so there was some wink-wink-wink going on behind the trip. McGill reached the same conclusion as I did, and began sliding away from the polar bears to the next pit. That left her only one pit away from the rear of the platform and the Andean bear.

Then came the bigger noise—of more than one car winding toward the plaza and of four suits, including the finicky man in brown, suddenly emerging from behind the raccoon cage. They came out in such a self-important rush I had a bad moment of thinking I was freezing before Paz and three henchmen. But they were just zoo suits or Bronx borough suits, so I went over for a better look at the arriving motorcade. Noisy it might have been, but it consisted only of a zoo security scooter, the limo, and the Bureau car with Hyde and Vincent.

Where the hell was Bernstein?

The limo followed the scooter into a space near the porcupine. The finicky man and his friends descended on the limo gingerly. Attracted by the commotion, people started gravitating toward the plaza. The coach kept telling his kids about polar bears, but a couple of them were more curious about the flags on Montaldo's car. A father with a toddler on his shoulders came around on the path that led back to the parking lot. A mother was suddenly cutting through the school group with a five- or six-year-old girl in hand. McGill began to go into overdrive just registering the new arrivals. I know she did because I did.

Montaldo came out of the limo with the same smile he'd had for the Bolivians at the church. The flack got out from the opposite side and gave another tug to his sleeves, as though he had just finished plastering on Montaldo's smile. He walked around the rear of the limo waiting to be noticed but didn't have much success until one of the zoo suits saw him standing outside the circle where Montaldo was being greeted. The flack smiled politely but not all that happily as he was brought into the group. Two possibilities occurred to me: He had a very proper sense of his own standing vis-a-vis Montaldo or he didn't want to be standing too close when the bullets started flying.

Then Vincent and Hyde got out of their car. I stepped back to a closed hot dog stand. How I had expected to stay anywhere near the ceremonies without being seen by them I had no idea.

The finicky man and Montaldo were all cordial conversation as they strolled toward the platform, now bedecked with American and Bolivian flags. A workman tapped the microphone, and his fingernail scratched the whole plaza. That was the last straw for the coach, who waved his group over to the ceremonies with a haste that gave away his own curiosity. McGill shot her eyes around wildly, then remembered where she was. She eased open the toggles on the front of her jacket.

My ferret moved back in, and this time with its family. I concentrated on getting behind Hyde and Vincent as they straggled after Montaldo and the welcoming committee. Maybe it was a jerk's move. If there had ever been a time to forget jurisdiction squabbling, this was it. But I continued to slink behind them. Down to it, I had no intention of offering the two creeps a last-second opportunity to change their tactics and come out as Montaldo's heroic saviors. They hadn't earned that public relations dividend. McGill had. Bernstein had. Jack Fine had. Even I had.

Bernstein must not have agreed. He suddenly appeared from the bear pit path, coming from the same direction as the school group had. With his haste and his sling there was no way the Feds could have missed him, and they didn't. Vincent faltered in his step, but Hyde stopped altogether. Hyde's face said he had never seen such arrogance before. He was apoplectic. Even Vincent was impressed enough by Hyde's reaction to stumble forward and whisper something in Bernstein's ear as they passed one another. Bernstein's answer was a roaring "fuck you!" over the plaza. The finicky man and the flack looked around blindly for the source of the disturbance, but some of the coach's kids traced it immediately and began giggling. It seemed as good a response as any.

Until the radio crackled in my pocket.

And then from somewhere inside Bernstein's overcoat.

It was Fine saying Curly and Dachshund had separated. Bernstein's look over to me gave me away to Hyde.

"One Rabbit is down," Fine said again, "and Turkey moving in your direction." The Connecticut cop seemed to have mastered McGill's code even less than I had, but I took him to mean that he had taken Dachshund out of action and that Curly was coming from the parking lot. But thanks to the swelling crowd surrounding the platform I couldn't see the path from the lot. The only one in that position was McGill, and I couldn't see her, either.

Bernstein held his ground, but Hyde came for me. His normal reptilian green was a purplish blister as he reached for my radio. "What the hell do you think you're playing at!"

If I hadn't knocked his arm away so hard, losing some balance in my shift, I wouldn't have seen Victor Paz as fast. He hadn't disguised himself in the least; he was the same string bean with salt-and-pepper hair from Nearing's photo, only now inside a blue down coat. And instead of from any of the six marked paths into the plaza, he was charging with a rapid, stagger-legged walk through what was probably shrubbery in the summer.

"Bernie!"

The finicky zoo man gave a tap to the microphone and removed some papers from his jacket pocket. The static blotted out my cry, but Bernstein saw enough on my face to turn around. He seemed to have an infinity of time to take in Paz and draw his weapon, so intent was Paz on stalking directly to the platform. But then the infinity ended: Paz hitched and saw Bernstein gaping at him. Bernstein had his coat open and his .9mm. in hand. Paz looked up at the platform uncertainly. There was a shout from someone around the lectern. Vincent was looking down from the platform. Hyde was cursing under his breath. Vincent grabbed Montaldo from the back of the waist and half-pulled, half-danced him away from the lectern.

Paz's gun was as big as a Magnum. He rolled his eyes into some place of desperation, then brought them down again into Bernstein and fired at the sling. "*Trampa! Trampa!*"

I knew he had to be shouting at Curly, but Curly was still somewhere behind the platform, out of my sight. I watched

Bernstein pat his mouth, as though trying to stop a hiccough. Paz was backing up again through the nonexistent shrubbery. I had my gun in my hand. There were shouts and screams as Bernstein crumpled. I blanked them out, told myself they were interfering. Nobody should have shouted because I was trying to prevent them from being hurt and they were making that harder for me.

A ping gashed asphalt and went off somewhere to the left. Hyde howled, then cursed some more. Bernstein got out of my way by landing fully on his sling. Victor Paz didn't know whether he wanted to retreat or keep shooting. There was panic in his eyes, but none in his fingers. Whatever was wrong with the leg that had given him a cranky forward motion when he walked, decided it: It balked under him. The Magnum-like thing came up crazily, leaving his throat wide open. Somebody was yelling my name from the platform, and I fired. Once. Twice. Three times. The first one caught Paz through the chin, and that was all I saw. He swiveled around so fast in the direction of the bear pits the other two shots had to have missed completely.

But he still didn't go down. Once the second and third bullets were beyond him, he came back to me. There was nothing between his nose and the top of his jacket, but the fingers were still in command.

My fourth shot took him down on the bridge of his nose. There had been nothing else to aim at, I told the piss in my pants.

And I repeated that aloud, hearing my dementia, to the voice that had been yelling at me from the platform. I knew it had been Frank Vincent's. He was the only one nodding to me.

* * *

Everything stank. I didn't dare get close to McGill while she tried to hold what was left of Bernstein in the cup of her hands. I didn't want to bend, either, so I'd have to feel the stink spreading up my body. McGill kept saying help was on the way, in the matter-of-fact way she said most things, but Bernstein wasn't buying. A dark blotch covered the front of his vest; not a bulletproof vest, but the lousy three-piece suit number he had worn just because his father and grandfather had. Sandy hair I've never noticed mussed before, not even after the highway crash, had developed wild, straggly ends. He kept gazing at her, waiting to hear the punchline to some joke she had started. So, where the hell was her sense of humor when it was really called for?

The plaza had been cleared. Those who had nothing valuable to say had been pushed behind a cordon that seemed to make half the animals in the zoo off limits. I'd seen them whisking Montaldo into an administration building, and for once the flack had run along practically begging for equal treatment with his boss. The litter was Paz, Curly, and Hyde.

And Bernstein.

Masterson came over to say the EMS had just driven through the gate. I heard his doubt and didn't give a damn about it. Maybe if he hadn't been so eager to help Fine in the parking lot with Dachshund—a situation Fine had already had under control—he could have been of more help. I didn't need his world-weary doubts.

And then it ended. McGill eased her hands down on the asphalt, then withdrew them from behind Bernstein's neck. Even the arm in the sling fell slack. I looked away so as not to have to see McGill. Vincent was talking on his car radio. A circle of blues was looking over at him; they seemed to be impressed by the way he had let his tie go askew or something. I got away from him before I said something stupid.

I ended up at the railing looking down at the Andean bear. A couple of security guards were singing McGill's praises for having taken out Curly with one shot. In a perfect world, I thought, she would have been flattered, but it wasn't a perfect world. The Andean bear—spectacled bear, black puma, whatever the hell it was called—would get its meals and not be hunted, but the tradeoff was the slapped together shale that was now its home. It was a double dose of prison: artificial *and* foreign.

Was the bear Phil Ortega's single Indio?

"Give me a cigarette."

McGill drooped her hands over the railing. She didn't move them again until I put a lighted cigarette in front of her face. She snatched at the smoke and looked away.

"Ask me something, Finley," she said after a moment.

I looked at the bear. It was peering up at us from a low ledge. Goddamn it if it didn't seem to be wondering what had happened to all the official ceremonies for its arrival!

I couldn't think of anything to ask having to do with an Andean bear. But then I did think of something. "What's *trampa* mean in Spanish?"

I thought she hadn't heard me, or hadn't heard Paz's shout and didn't know what I was talking about. But then the cigarette dropped from her hand into the pit. The bear looked interested, but only for a second. "Trap," she said, her voice quivering from somewhere inside my throat.

NINE

I tried to make peace with the lies; there wasn't much I could have done about most of them anyway. The hardest to accept was the one midwifed by Hilary Davenport. It was Hilary Davenport, a tourist from Ann Arbor, who had been shooting Montaldo with her Canon X-Something as Vincent had pulled the ambassador out of harm's way—a shot that ended up on the front page of the *Times* and *USA Today* and that brought her invitations to all the morning talk shows. Vincent flanked her for all appearances, getting out the word that, even at the cost of brave agents like William Hyde, the FBI remained scrupulous about its duty to protect citizen and non-citizen alike. Nobody was more appreciative of that trust than Montaldo, who received Vincent a couple of days later to confer a medal and voice the gratitude of the Bolivian people that the FBI had saved their official representative.

In calmer moments, I had to admit Vincent deserved acknowledgment for thinking so fast on his feet. Whether because he had been operating under a deliberately ambiguous directive, because Hyde had been standing at some distance at the critical second, or because a trained instinct had taken over, Vincent *had* made a choice. Why there had to have been one to make . . . Well, that was when my calm receded again.

With Vincent and Hyde so dedicated to their oaths, everybody else came out as the supporting cast. Jack Fine barely made that status. In the interests of atoning to the NYPD for Vincent's stardom, the grayheads reviewing the fiasco reversed the roles of Fine and Masterson in subduing Dachshund in the parking lot. As soon as he got the drift, Fine called me from Connecticut to ask if I'd back him in setting the record straight. But as soon as I said I would, he switched gears by reminding me I hadn't been in the lot when he had moved against Dachshund, so why should anyone believe what I had to say? We left that riddle to the long-distance operator for a few seconds, then he came back on the line to thank me and hang up. I haven't heard from him since and sometimes think he had mainly called for my reassurances that he had been in the zoo that day.

Not even the grayheads could manipulate Bernstein and Mc-Gill out of the picture; not entirely, anyway. Bernstein drew a posthumous assignment as head of a "special NYPD unit" working in cooperation with the Feds to guard Montaldo. A brother from Ohio came to receive the department's condolences and was center stage for the inspector's funeral. For her part, McGill never opened her mouth, even walking away from a battery of TV microphones after receiving her own decoration, ignoring the mayor's wave to say a few words. But mute as she was, she was present for everything public having to do with Bernstein. Silence had never been so relentless or so eloquent: She simply wasn't going to be trifled with. At the inspector's funeral, her whole body seemed to have been fitted into her white gloves, and whether snapping off a salute or glancing at the brother from Canton standing next to her, she exuded total control. I wasn't surprised to read a short time later she had been "promoted" to an administrative position in Homicide Analysis. It sounded like a job that, behind the gloss of rewarding her, would keep her away from superiors with uneasy consciences.

And then there was me.

I didn't have Fine's vulnerable jurisdiction problem or McGill's sang-froid. What I did have was a tumor of angers so obvious that several batteries of debriefers tried to use it to erase me from the picture altogether. Naturally, this only made my tumor expand further.

The first team, from the local Bronx precinct, was obsessed with such cosmic questions as my gun license and why I had chosen to park near the firehouse instead of in the zoo lot. Only when a captain showed up did we get down to my relationship with Bernstein and other members of that "special NYPD unit." The captain left me sitting in a back room of the station house until the second team arrived from Police Plaza.

The second team was from Special Investigations, and the beginning and end of progress was that I didn't hear any more questions about licenses and parking choices. Their pet theme was how I had taken it into my head that the only way to incapacitate "the unidentified Hispanic male we have" was to shoot him. When I pointed out that Bernstein and Hyde had already been cut down by the unidentified Hispanic male they had, that the unidentified Hispanic male they had had continued firing, and that the unidentified Hispanic male they had wouldn't have been so unidentified if they bothered to talk to Frank Vincent or anyone working at the Bolivian mission, we moved on. For instance, to my skills as a physician able to diagnose from so far away that Bernstein had been shot and to the extraordinary peripheral vision that had enabled me to tell Hyde had taken a bullet. They were about to take their sledgehammers to that enthralling flaw in my story when I dug out the business card of Mrs. Morgan's lawyer. They were aghast. How could I have misread my situation so badly? There was no need for lawyers, they were just trying to get the facts straight for the record. They left me alone in the back room for another half-hour, but they also had a deskman bring me a coffee and a cruller.

The collar pins alone would have told me where the third team had come from, but I didn't need to piece together frail clues. I recognized the lineman from the Ciera parked across the street from the Bolivian mission. Bob Cicotte I knew from the federal prosecutor's office years before and, since then, from all those self-important TV press conferences that took place in the libraries of East Side mansions.

An ascetic, humorless man who seemed suited for a monk's cell, Cicotte cut right to the chase. He would be the first to go outside and sing my praises to the media; if I hadn't acted when I had, Agent Vincent and Ambassador Montaldo might have met the same end as Agent Hyde. Then, too, he was aware of some "sloppiness" in the Bureau's surveillance of Montaldo; just the fact that zoo security hadn't been put on special alert asked for an investigation. But what I also had to understand was that there was more involved than an assassination attempt and—God help him for saying it—a couple of dead law enforcement people. Had I considered the diplomatic ramifications, not only vis-a-vis the Bolivians but regarding the whole United Nations? These were not petty concerns.

He went on for about ten minutes, with the lineman producing a loyal nod with every new factor mentioned. I was exhausted just listening—the perfect state from his point of view for the topper. "And let's not forget another thing, Paul. We start delving into the roles various agencies played here and the media's going to forget about the Martian theory of who killed Kennedy and make life miserable for anyone who ever heard of Victor Paz or even talked to anyone who ever heard of him."

I thought about the homeless man who had been studying the stock tables at McDonald's, then about the woman in the running suit. Then I had to think about the Professor's buddy Roger Nearing. What the gods dispensed, they took back once their purpose had been served. Was it entirely impossible that Cicotte was delivering a message from Nearing himself, that I had run out of usefulness for McDonald's meetings?

"See our situation, Paul? This could lead to a whole lot of people who won't appreciate having their lives interrupted."

"What are you asking?"

What he was asking was "reasonableness." And being as confident as he was of acquiring it, he could set out all its features in technicolor for me right away. Aside from the honors formula for the Feds and the NYPD, there was the fortuitousness of my having happened along as Paz had begun firing, my shock at seeing Bernstein and Hyde go down, and my instinct for self-defense in taking out Paz. There would, of course, be public acknowledgment of my efforts—along the lines of that given the first rescuer on the scene in Lakehurst, New Jersey after the *Hindenburg* had gone down. If I could abstain from all but the most generic remarks to the media, that would show I was as reasonable as everyone else caught up in the "complex situation" and earn me a gold star with Federal agencies, in particular, those that might prove of use to a private investigator.

Except for being ready to renege on the deal during Jack Fine's call and skipping Montaldo's award ceremonies, I showed reasonableness. Since none of the reporters had an inkling about address books, Panamanian coins, or drivers running amok on New England turnpikes, I mostly had to answer questions about my police career in Mineola and my investigation work in Brooklyn, and how these two career stops had prepared me for being a modern Buffalo Bill. One son of a bitch preferred dwelling on the two shots that had missed Paz and how I might have felt if I had killed a child, but Cicotte finally intervened to turn the prick's tabloid background against him. Given my compromising state of mind, I found it natural to attend Bernstein's funeral as just another body in the crowd.

For about three-and-a-half minutes I persuaded myself I was doing my spineless act in the Professor's name. The next layer down—crasser than the Joe Carroll ledge—was that, thanks to my new sharpshooting fame, Finley Investigations had only booming times ahead. Well, not quite. For a week or so the answering machine ran out of tape every day. After weeding out the interview requests, the jerks wanting to check if I was the same Paul Finley, and a few cranks who wanted to know how I felt about the National Rifle Association and U.S. immigration policies toward Latin America, I had eight more clients. Nothing to sneeze at, but not adding up to Bernstein, Rosemary, Olmos, and the Mirandas, either.

And then there was the third level: those endless seconds back in the zoo when I had frozen up. The tabloid guy had had it backward since the threat to others hadn't been in the shots I had fired, but in the ones I had let Paz fire. Frank Vincent had made up his mind about what to do in three or four seconds, I had needed three times that long. Had that been the difference for Hyde? The doubt wormed itself in and kept wriggling.

And what about Bernstein? Why had he been so slow to react? Every time I replayed the scene in my mind I saw the fat man's gun in his ham hand and doing nothing. Where had all the hesitation come from? Not from his collarbone, not from lack of experience. In the end, I had to accept that, despite all the choices and subterfuges that had gone into tracking him, when the time had come, neither Bernstein nor I had been ready for the real Victor Paz. In the few seconds it had been critical to believe in the man as a flesh and blood threat, as more than a figment of our police minds and target of personal scores, Victor Paz—as Lerico might have said—had remained beyond our comprehension.

* * *

Not even one of the telephone messages was from the Professor. I called him the afternoon of the shootings, warned him what to expect on the TV news and promised to call again when I had my head back together. He went along far more scrupulously than I had expected; since my move from his place to Brooklyn, it was the first time we had allowed a week to go by without touching base. Both of us knew our next talk would revolve around Roger Nearing, and I was no more eager for it than he was.

We finally had it one night after my class. The class had been my first since being sequestered at the Ramada Inn, and I wouldn't have been surprised to find an empty room waiting for me. Instead, the kids treated my absence as some practical field work in law enforcement and assailed me with eager questions. I stuck to the Cicotte line, hating myself every word of the way. Less than a half-hour into the session I couldn't take my evasions anymore and walked out with a promise to be "more myself" the next time. The prospect of having that jerk in greater bloom put me in the perfect mood for seeing the Professor.

I don't know which one of us sighed more when he opened the door. "Always exciting to have a TV star in the house," he recovered, leaving me to close the door while he trudged back to his living room lounger. "Get yourself a drink. I'm on the last chapter of something."

I took my time hanging my coat in the hall closet, then went into the kitchen and poured a Dewar's over ice as slowly as I could. The fact was, I didn't want to ask him anything; what I really wanted was to walk out into the living room and have him hit me with everything before I said a word.

I almost got my wish. "I don't think Brook Farm was exactly what Fourier was aiming for," he said, clapping his book closed and setting it on the table next to him. "Then again you have to wonder if utopians have ever known what they're aiming for."

"Maybe it's all in the trip getting there."

"Maybe. I thought your class ended at eight."

"The teacher was indisposed."

"Oh." He rattled the cubes in what looked to be tonic water or club soda. "Fire away."

"How about you just tell me?"

"That important to you?"

"You asked me to ask only if it was."

He smiled ruefully. "Stupid me. Your imagination must be running riot. Who am I—that guy in *I Led Three Lives*?"

"I'll settle for what I don't know about the first one."

He said nothing for a moment, then lifted his heavy legs up on the hassock with a grunt. "I had a little problem on campus some years ago," he said, keeping his eyes averted. "Right after Nixon and Kissinger decided the peaceful way to get out of Vietnam was to rip apart Cambodia. We weren't as boisterous as some universities, but we had our demonstrations. I had something to say at a couple of them, and that didn't go over too well. I didn't give a damn. I had tenure. I had the right to say what even *Time* and *Newsweek* were getting up the nerve to say. I was the head of the department. What were they going to do—replace me?"

"Probably."

"Well, they sure as hell tried. Give me a cigarette."

"They're not good for you."

"And for you they're vitamins. Give me one."

I did, he took a puff, then examined the cigarette between his thick fingers as if it had latched on to him without warning. "The first time they called me on the carpet, they were all civility. So was I. I was far too clever to tell them just to go to hell. What I told them instead was they were short-sighted, that somebody like me was their best guarantee of keeping things under control, prevent another Kent State."

"Did you believe it?"

"A little. There was an emotion in some of those demos, Paul, that scared the bejesus out of me. Some part of me wanted to believe very badly I could still control things. I was as terrified as the administration and board of trustees. People, especially kids, weren't supposed to be that passionate about anything. What else could it lead to but chaos?"

"Persuade the administration?"

He burped a laugh into his glass. "I thought I had. But then a couple of days later I got up in the cafeteria during a rally and told everyone about how I'd been summoned to account for myself. Maybe I just got caught up in the moment. Maybe I saw too much passion and sincerity in front of me and not nearly enough in my own head. There was a call for a sit-in, and I supported it. That not only got the school back on my case but was too tempting to some of the people in my department. There were three of them—all believers in Edmund Burke as the Second Coming and all drooling to get my chair. They all had a favorite trustee for reporting my latest insult to God and Flag. Your mother-in-law and I used to bet which one of them would come up with the best new accusation before sundown."

"Jennifer never mentioned any of this."

"Because she didn't know about it! Oh, I suppose she sensed tension around the house and heard I wasn't the flavor of the month on campus. But she was a high school teenager with her own problems. Anyway, it all came to a head when I was supposed to attend a history conference in London. Two weeks before I was scheduled to leave I was informed my services would be required for a budget meeting of department heads, so best I cancel those tickets to England. Funny, but my department was the only one that heard about this urgent budget meeting. So, I said no, I was going over to the conference. Prancing right into mismanagement charges. That was when the FBI called. Character named Bell."

"For what?"

"Nothing special, he said. But could I drop around to his office and answer a few questions? I told him to go screw himself."

He had done everything right, I thought, polishing off my scotch. Roger Nearing still didn't fit.

"But Bell's call unnerved me. Made me mad, too. So, I had a little talk with the editor of the campus newspaper. Bright kid, did a brilliant paper for me on Charlemagne in Spain . . ."

"Joe!"

"Okay, okay. The kid couldn't write it all down fast enough. He was envisioning a Pulitzer. Too bad for him my timing was off. See, he was only a few days away from graduation and had practically passed the editor's baton on to his successor. When the last spring issue came out, there was no interview. The kid said he didn't know what'd happened, he'd left it with his successor because the new staff was doing the last issue. I called up the new editor—an English major, as I remember—and he didn't know what the hell I was going on about. To this day I don't think he was lying. Someone just swiped the thing. Odd coincidence, but Bell came me again right after that. No more politeness. Told me I wasn't doing myself or my family any good with the things I was going around saying. I swear he was reading my quotes from the campus paper story."

"There are bigger papers than a college weekly."

He finally tired of watching the cigarette burn down in his hand, and squashed it in the ashtray on the table. "For a crusader ready to go the whole nine yards I suppose there are," he said testily. "But I was mainly just pissed off, and after that story vanished I didn't even have much energy for that. I withdrew into my shell. Everybody was to blame—Bell, the kid who'd done the story, the one who said he never saw it, Nixon, Kissinger. I didn't trust anybody. That's when Nearing came along."

I was abruptly back to me and hadn't realized how comfortable I had been not being there.

"Through a trustee named Gregory Franz. Big Democrat, real estate in the Hamptons. Franz came up to me before graduation and slapped me on the shoulder, said not to worry, everything he'd been hearing would blow over. Then he suggests I meet this friend of his." He swung his legs off the hassock. "Confession may be great for the soul, son-in-law, but it doesn't do much for the tongue. Your glass."

I let him waddle into the kitchen by himself, thinking I wanted another drink more than the rest of the story. What could he have told me that had ended up worse than the bloodbaths at the Miranda home and the zoo? His yarn was Casbah cafe crap; just replace Sydney Greenstreet's fez with Joe Carroll's mortarboard. What did it have to do with Bernstein and Rosemary Stanton being killed? I didn't like how the photo of Jennifer and Susan atop the TV set seemed to scold me for not having figured it out.

He came back with two scotches and stayed on his feet near the bookcase. "No problem at all, Roger Nearing said. Did I want to go to London for that conference? So go. If there was any trouble, he'd talk to some alumni for me. It was the 1970s, for Christ sake!"

"He's lost a little of that élan."

The Professor smiled. "A crossword puzzle word." He took too big a swallow. "Of course I could help him, too. And I didn't tell him to go screw himself like I'd told Bell. I didn't have a phone between us, so there went half my courage right there. Plus, I was just worn out, Paul. With the school, all those backstabbers in my department, even the students. Know the only things I thought I had left?"

"Your wife and Jennifer."

"Them, of course." He waited a moment out of decency to get back to the answer he had intended originally. "Plus History. History with a capital H. The present was a shithole? Okay, but I still had my subject. Nobody could take that away. And that's what I betrayed more than anything."

"I don't understand."

"All he asked me to do was what I'd planned to do anyway," he said impatiently. "Go to London, read my paper, hit every restaurant in Soho. The one extra—the one that would guarantee I'd have a department to come back to—was to get what he called an 'informal sense' of what the other people at the conference thought of adventures like Cambodia."

"He needed *you* for that?"

"Of course he didn't. What he needed from me was a frame of mind. Salesmen have customer quotas, cops have arrest quotas, and the Nearings have pawn quotas."

"So you gave him this reading on the other historians."

"I can remember it to this day," he said, flopping back down in his lounger. "Yapp in Utrecht had regular contacts with the Vietnamese in Paris. Ciattini never missed a demonstration organized by the Italian Left. Dracovic in Belgrade was worried a prolonged war in Asia would embolden the Soviets in Europe. Ingels at Cambridge wanted his Tory lords and masters to pull back from total support of Nixon. I got every one of their views down and I gave it to Nearing in a tidy little report with a cellophane cover. I think he was dismayed by the cellophane cover."

He fell silent, gazing over the rim of his glass to the television. I thought of all the evenings he had spent back at the old house watching old movies. Had he merely turned on *Some Like It Hot* because it wouldn't have interfered with remembering how he had once worked for Roger Nearing?

"How did you get out from under, Joe?"

"You assume I did."

"Yeah, I do."

He blinked, looking not quite grateful. "I played myself off the damn chessboard, that's how. The one advantage to being empty inside is being able to tell yourself you have nothing to lose. You get nerve you usually don't have. Something to replace what you've bartered away." He shook his head in bafflement, then shot me a glare. "Need a diagram? I got as far as making up an excuse to get Ruth out of the house. Then I went into the garage and padded all the cracks with rags."

It was the first since the accident I was glad Jennifer couldn't be part of our conversation. "But you couldn't do it."

"Why do you think that was?"

"I don't care why."

His face erupted like a blister. "Do care, Finley! Because I can tell you it had nothing to do with a bureaucratic creep like Roger Nearing! Roger Nearing didn't send me into that garage and he sure as hell didn't get me out of it! Start crediting those guys with that kind of power and they've really beaten you!"

"Then why?"

He was disappointed not to get more of an argument. "What I said before—withdrawing into my shell, feeling threatened by everything around me. The ones who drove me into that cave? My own students, that's who. Not Roger Nearing, but teenagers who didn't even read the *Times* Book Review. It was what they had in their heads that jeopardized the Professor's tenure. The retreat into fear, that was in this head long before Mr. Roger Nearing came along. That was my real betrayal, Paul ---trying to curl up and go to sleep inside the goddamn Treaty of Versailles!"

"Your vanity?"

He laughed at the look on my face. "Don't underrate it. The first time I have to think of history as more than academic memory and here I am sticking rags under a garage door! Don't you love the mockery of it? What a fine teacher I'd been for those kids—living my entire professional life scared shitless of my own specialization!"

I sipped my scotch only to blunt his stare. He was probably telling me more than he had ever told anybody, but I still felt manipulated in some way. "You were about to tell me how you got away from Nearing."

He nodded in approval. "Finley the cop."

"What did you do about Nearing, Joe?"

He glanced at a framed photo of Ruth Carroll on the bookshelf; she was standing in a beret and short skirt near a pier, looking apprehensive she might fall into the water behind her. "That was her reaction, too, when I told her about the garage. She must've been trembling in every bone of her body, but she pretended she wasn't even surprised. She wanted to make it seem obvious I had to dig myself out of the hole I'd made. She made me want to make her right, Finley. I couldn't wait to meet Gregory Franz, to tell him about my almost-event. He turned white, whiter, whitest. Clearly, I'd become unreliable as a pawn. Who knew what I might say or do next? Name him as a friend of Nearing's, maybe? That wasn't his image, not among his liberal friends. I thought I'd overdone it, made myself another enemy on the board. But no, he was too vulnerable and I was too clearly troubled. And then we had peace in our time and no more Roger Nearing."

He was telling a story, only a story, I thought, in which despair and attempted suicide were things that had happened to Joe Carroll the way they might have once happened to a Confederate general or a Middle Ages tinker. I was still missing something.

"Saw a shrink a few times. But what it came down to was I had to get back to what I knew how to do—teaching. And not history as some kind of recent archeology, but as an ongoing process."

"You mean it was safe to come out again. The protest signs had been put back in the warehouse."

He winced; it had come out more nastily than I had intended. "That's one way of looking at it, I guess. I also got rid of those three stooges in my department. My prerogative and I used it. Think I should've done more?"

The penny dropped. "You did do more, Joe. Nearing said you did. What did he mean?"

"More?"

"He wouldn't have just said it. The guy weighs every word, sells it by the letter. He was referring to something specific."

He started to shake his head, but then stopped. He wanted to laugh, then had second thoughts. "Don't you see it?"

"See what?"

"*You*, Paul—you're the more!"

I knew immediately he was right. I hadn't gotten the punchline to the little joke outside McDonald's because I had been too busy thinking up my prank about chasing after him to the subway.

"The bastard," the Professor muttered. "With some pawns, I guess you take the long view."

I felt numb as I watched him lift his glass. I tried picturing him drinking his scotch in the Wooden Quarter, across the street from the High Note, but couldn't do it. I knew it was more than just the difference in scotch glasses making it impossible.

"Admit you're impressed, Paul," he said uneasily.

"We're not talking about us."

"We're not?"

"It's not about any secrets from yesteryear, what we have or haven't made of them since," I heard myself saying. "It's about a lot of people still getting killed because we value those little secrets, keep them in our little invisible places, and take them out only when we hope we can be admired for them."

Alarm passed through his stare but kept going. "You feel that strongly about it, you should do something about it."

"Right. The only trouble with that, according to Angela, is I'm the same thing as what I'm against."

"Smart woman. That's why I've admitted her to my circle. Of course, she could also be full of shit."

Down to it, I didn't want to walk out on him so curtly. But then he turned away from me ever so deliberately to put his glass on the end table. "Don't forget to call, huh?"

"Right."

When I turned back to close the front door after me, he was already in communion with the TV. It sounded like a commercial for frozen pizza.

* * *

Letting the Nearings of the world think I was a continuous pawn for them was harder to swallow than the compromises I had agreed to with Cicotte. But I still I wasted some time directing my determination to show unreasonable I could be. Angela took the brunt of my first, easy attack. Who the hell was she, after all? Was it just a coincidence she had moved in with the Ortegas when the Paz affair had begun and had moved out again when Ortega had admitted how my name had gotten into the address book? Who believed in coincidences? And who was to say Argentina didn't have all kinds of shadowy interests in what went on in Bolivia? They were both South American countries, weren't they? And was it just another of those famous coincidences that their names began with the first two letters of the alphabet? And another thing, wasn't she just a little bit too philosophical for somebody whose field was political science?

She didn't think so. In fact, she didn't think there was anything the least theoretical about telling a budding paranoid to go fuck himself. Either did I. I aimed my resentment elsewhere.

We saw each other about once a week until she finished her project and returned to Buenos Aires. In the best of times, we knew we were heading for the same place, and could wrap ourselves in each other with an excitement for that fact. The rest of the time, especially after my Kafka spells, it was only too obvious that, even heading for the same place, we were going there on parallel tracks. I left her the knowledge of the joke about the cop on Kosciusko Street and the promise to answer at once her letters about how she and La Boca were changing, and she left me with tapes of Astor Piazzolla and much less acne.

Little by little, my aim at Nearing becoming truer, I told my class about Allen Bernstein, Rosemary Stanton, and Hector Miranda. When I was feeling optimistic, I envisioned some of the kids raising embarrassing questions in Ortega's classes. When I was feeling pessimistic, I saw Ortega congratulating them for their interest in Latin American politics and referring them to one of his books for further study.

Beyond those two possibilities? Well, there was the fact that, while I had been describing my first meeting at McDonald's with Roger Nearing, one of the bozos in the back had seemed less fascinated by the impression his watchband had left on his wrist. I liked the idea that, for a couple of minutes anyway, I had learned something about teaching some of the practical problems of law enforcement.

www.ingramcontent.com/pod-product-compliance
Lightning Source LLC
Chambersburg PA
CBHW030515260626
47157CB00005B/1746